LEGENDS of AZUREIGN:

The COMPACT SHATTERS

Joy Oestreicher

Omega Cat Press — California

Omega Cat Press, independent publishing since 1990

Paperback ISBN: 978-1-954225-18-3

Hardcover ISBN: 978-1-954225-19-0

Electronic Book ISBN: 978-1-954225-20-6

1 2 3 4 5 6 7 8 9

For Samantha, fondly known to her parents as the energizer bunny, who has dived into life headfirst, willing to see and try, willing to do and be:

May you find amazement and happiness in your seeking; peace and joy in your achievements.

Table of Contents

MAP: Azureign

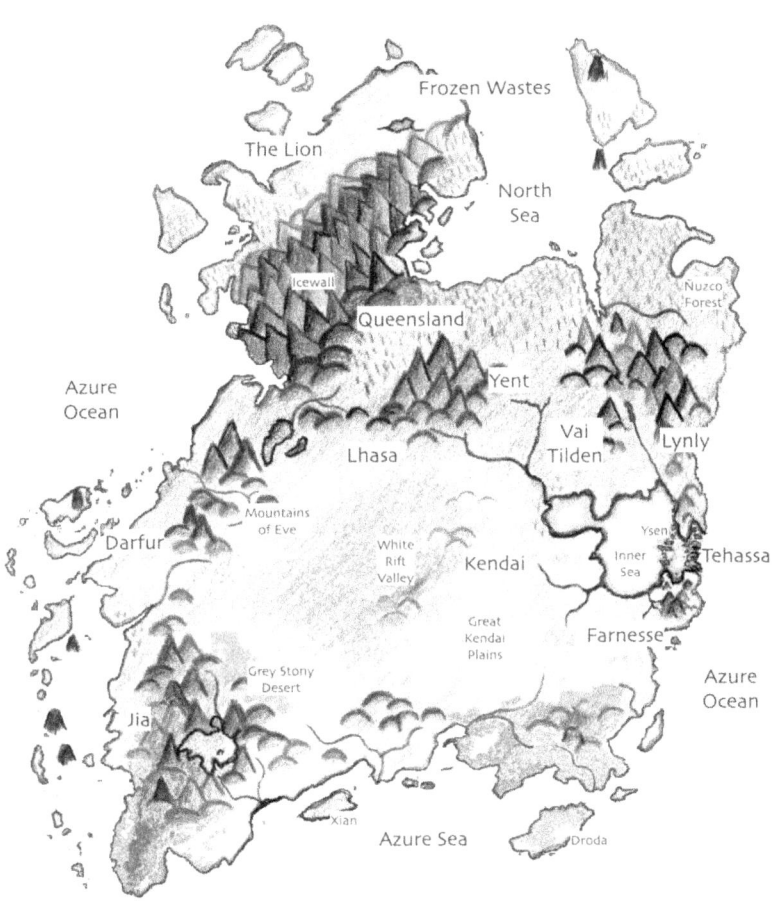

Frozen Wastes

The Lion

North Sea

Icewall

Queensland

Nuzco Forest

Azure Ocean

Yent

Vai Tilden

Lynly

Lhasa

Mountains of Eve

White Rift Valley

Kendai

Ysen

Inner Sea

Tehassa

Darfur

Great Kendai Plains

Farnesse

Grey Stony Desert

Azure Ocean

Jia

Xian

Azure Sea

Droda

AZUREIGN

MAP: Tehassa

INTERVAL: The Ayi Representative

By comparison with other wars in the universe, the Azureign rebellion was not amounting to much— except for those directly involved, including myself.

But in the minds of at least three of our fellow Compact members, *Toridani, Simbara* and especially *Mengsee,* it is a disaster. Disaster, for a single shining reason: It is confirming that the Compact has flaws. Its designers are imperfect and their results are likewise imperfect.

Plus, this has happened before. The end result of the species' *Jackqua*'s revolt was their leaving the Compact. They are almost an enemy now, who could have been allies.

Somehow that is not convincing the Mengsee. They still try to change the people, ignoring millions of years of evolution. It is not the various peoples that have been created wrongly. It is the Mengsee's idea at fault. And the Compact's.

The Compact must change.

These facts are frightening the Compact members I mention above, beyond all common sense.

I am thinking this is one of the reasons any interdictions by the Compact should be overseen by *all* Compact members, not just a select few, who might have their own biases or agendas in each case. Certainly the Mengsee must not be allowed to interfere again.

But who am I to be judging these things?

My name is Dzarn Reith Koras. I am guard (and backup navigator) to Lady Dzarn Calindey Ashaza, who has brought her ship *Star Glow* to Azureign to assist the colonists, both Humanity and Dolphinfolk.

My species, *Ayi,* is having only one vote in Compact matters. Any member can be easily outvoted by the shifting coalitions among other Compact members. In the issue of Humanity, we have been outvoted. Regarding Humanity's colony Azureign, we have been outvoted even more profoundly and consistently.

We are not supposed to interfere with this interdicted planet, or these people upon it. Never mind how those three other species are already involved in interference here.

So we Ayi who are trying to help must be sneaking in and offering aid as invisibly as we can. What the result will be, I cannot guess, but I can hope it is in favor of the Humans and Dolphinfolk here.

I am chosen to be an interface with the family K!elli!, (called Kell for easier pronouncing, we are told) in the Azureign nation of Tehassa.

I would rather be back on my Lady's ship.

Not only am I alone, I must contrive to stay hidden even while I listen and advise the nation's leadership to set up this war, and help to guide them through their early days after they—presumably—leave the Compact.

But I am putting the *cart* before the *horse,* as the Humans say. First came the rebellion itself.

—Dzarn Reith Koras, of
Calindey's *Star Glow*

Chapter One: Conflagration

Loud noises and shouts outside my suite windows woke me. I stumbled out of my bed and yanked back the heavy curtains. Across the yard I saw angry red flames that tinted the sky a ghastly grey-pink. I looked down to see servants, guards, and Ras Zola—my sister—all running toward the blazing hangar.

I rushed to pull on heavy linen pants and a shirt I'd dropped on the floor the night before and then made my way downstairs and outside, toward the fire, where it seemed half the city's population gathered to make a bucket brigade.

"Zeden!" my sister yelled. I waved at her.

I saw her join the bucket-brigade line. My one-year older sister always seemed to go before me in everything. Perhaps I am just slow.

As I arrived at the fire, a pumper wagon arrived also. Pulled by a pair of placid oxen—our horses are notoriously unreliable in fires—it rolled up, stopped, and several of the bucket crew switched to the pumper.

Two big men yanked the hose into position and opened the stopcock. I noticed drips from leaks in several spots. I made a note to fix those or get a new tank for the pumper. We keep it near the stables for just such emergencies; it wasn't going to help if all the water runs out before we need to use it.

I was so intent on the pumper that I stumbled over a broken bucket that had been tossed aside. I watched my feet more carefully as I stepped forward to assist the young woman on one side of the pumper frame. I'm not overly large but I am strong. I could help balance the huge man working the other side of the see-saw contraption. Of course, our large solar-powered fire trucks would arrive eventually, but this little pumper was more effective than buckets. We could keep a stream of water going up strong enough to hit the roof.

It was our balloon hangar that burned. Thousands of meters of balloon silk were laid out on the floor, ready to be fastened to each lightweight plass basket over the next few days. A group of our balloons is being sent to help distract the aliens at the Compact's Oracle installation when the rebel ships attack the Preserve.

I kept my suspicions to myself, but it didn't take a genius to figure out the fire must be arson—set by someone who objected to Father's plan to join the multi-national revolt against our alien overseers.

My family's ancestors had signed the Compact agreement *over a thousand years ago.* They had assumed at that time that Azureign's interdiction would eventually be lifted, and the planet's settlers would then be free of alien intervention and their alien —and limiting—rules.

Now we wonder: How long is *eventually?*

How long must we follow the aliens' strictures? Supposedly the rules keep us Humans from further wrecking the planet's biomes (many species in the Compact had been horrified that Azureign had been terraformed). But in practice, it was more like rules to keep us all landbound and primitive compared to the rest of the galaxy, and for far too long: Here was Azureign a millennium later, still under alien control, still putting out fires with pumper wagons. It was as absurd as it was cruel.

The ringing sound in my ears transformed into the big fire truck's bell-and-siren, as one of the city's two "modern" trucks arrived. The girl and I continued to pump, unconsciously matching our rhythm to the ring of the bell. Every three dings, push, rest for three more dings as we let the bar rise back up from the push by the enormous man on the other side, then for three dings we pushed again.

The driver of the big truck jumped out. "Ras Zeden," she said to me, "the second truck is still filling up."

I nodded to her, continuing to pump. The big trucks go to suck up water from the Inner Sea as it roars past our islands before plunging down the Falls at the Edge of the World into the Azure Ocean far below.

The one thing Tehassa has plenty of is water, fresh on the inner side, mild salt on the outer.

Once the big truck got its two hoses going, the fire visibly diminished. The flames were gone by the time the second truck arrived, but they stayed to help. We all worked together to drown every speck of ember, every ash and soot coating that might be hiding coals that could rise again.

I walked with the fire captain around the remains of the building, ensuring all sparks were out, and to see what, if anything, was left of our people's hard work. We were joined by my sister, who had been in the bucket brigade that had moved to the back side of the hangar. She met my gaze before turning back to stare at the remnants of our balloon skirmish vehicles.

Soot greyed Zola's skin and lightened her hair; smears of ash coated her arms and her workout clothes. Like her, I must be coated in ash. Like me, she'd apparently grabbed whatever clothes had lain nearby and rushed outside.

Neither of us was even wearing shoes.

"Quite the royal pair, aren't we?" she murmured.

"Did anyone see who set this?" I asked.

The fire captain glanced back and forth between us two siblings, his expression startled. "You think it's arson?" he asked.

Zola cleared her throat. She always seized the chance to speak first. I closed my mouth. Let her say it. I might be Eze one day, but I hoped to have her help in speaking to others. I am not good at it. She is. We both know this.

I am good at other things, like logistics, tactics, anything that can be assembled using the language of mathematics. Also puzzles and conundrums. But like my feet, my mouth didn't seem to work if my mind was concentrating on a problem.

Sometimes I wonder if Father—the Eze (our king)—ever regrets the patrilineal inheritance laws of our nation. It seems to me that he, along with most our people, thought Zola would do a better job of eventually ruling our nation than I. It is an ancient system, brought with us from Earth. Perhaps if I ever do become Eze, it is a thing I can change.

"You lack focus," my tutor once said. But in my view, my problem is the very opposite: I focus on one issue *too much;* so thoroughly in fact, it is like the rest of the universe just vanishes from consideration. All my attention is on the current problem, not on constructing a verbal response. Or watching where my feet go.

"It's almost certainly arson," Zola said. "In protest to us joining the revolution against the Compact, I suppose."

The fire captain shook his head. "People don't like change," he said. "But to destroy the work of so many, to burn up all that silk—that's crazy, too. What a waste!"

I hid my smile. The man believed a revolt against the Compact was *crazy,* but more than that, he deplored the *waste* the protestors had made. How many others felt the same?

Father had asked us—Zola and me—to get a sense of the people's feelings about a possible revolt, months ago. We found that many of our people strongly resented the Compact's restrictive rules. Most Tehassan citizens felt it was time to break the Compact.

They wanted to be free.

They yearn to have the advantages of higher technology we had recently learned could be available to us. Especially, there are medical advances we all believe the rest of Humanity in the galaxy has, that we do not.

Our scientists and medics have discovered a few helpful things, which we have kept hidden from the Compact observers as well as we can; they might take them away.

We also have added some simple herbal cures people had found in the Library of Humanity—the secret resource our ancestors hid away at the time of Azureign's interdiction. The Library and all the information it held had been recently rediscovered. Besides being a treasure trove for all the peoples of Azureign, it opened our eyes. The Compact aliens have held us back so long, we are like cavemen.

For example, inoculations against diseases mankind had abolished from the face of Earth millennia ago still attacked and killed our people here on Azureign. These cures are not innovative. Their preparation is not going to damage Azureign's ecology. Yet such things are forbidden by the Compact. Or perhaps only by the aliens who oversee Azureign.

The people who are afraid to break from the Compact do not think about these restrictions. They do not consider the benefits we would gain from having a normal level of research and technology.

Instead they are *rabid* with fear. Fear of the Compact aliens and what they might do to us if we break their cruel rules.

Their argument: "That's what the Compact promises," the opposition leaders had published in a broadside: "*All Humans will be removed for eternity if there is war or Compact limitations are broken.*"

That was the point the Opposition to the revolt shouted in the streets. We would be removed from Azureign.

And they were right. We *could* be taken from Azureign. We could be made homeless among the stars. But was that worse than staying here with only the tech levels of millennia ago?

Besides, no matter how valid anyone's arguments are, the attack is *going to happen*. With Tehassa or without us.

Our contribution to the effort would make it more likely to succeed, but many, many others were involved, not just our own peoples.

If our nation withdrew, or even opposed the rebellion, we cannot make *the others* stop. Especially we cannot stop the Dolphinfolk, who are sincerely determined to free themselves.

The protestors refused to support the war effort with their money, goods or people, arguing their intention to stay neutral.

Neutral!

The more I thought about it, the angrier I got. Is it a *neutral* act to set fire to a shed full of hot air balloons? I shook my head. It didn't make any more sense to me than the Opposition itself did. How could they think their little revolt inside a revolt would save us? How did they imagine their *neutrality* would protect them? It certainly wasn't going to stop the war.

Neither would burning up our balloon fleet.

The fire captain used his staff to poke at a clump of ash, breaking it apart. It was cold and wet and held no spark: extinguished. Safe.

"It could have been worse," he said. We have a few minor burns, but no lives were lost."

Zola nodded in agreement, but I did not respond. I hate it when people say, "Things could be worse." Because it seems that then things always, always *do* get worse. As if the Universe can't stand to let the statement go unchallenged.

Our alien Ayi observer—or liaison, as *his* leader had called him—said nothing about the fire that had destroyed so many balloon envelopes. As I supervised the cleanup, I saw him pick up buckets and help put things back in order. All without a word.

The young man, called Reith Koras, seldom says anything at all. He just watches us, watches what we do and say, with his leaf-green eyes bright with curiosity. Sometimes it's kind of creepy.

He did say once that part of his job was to further his understanding and competence with our language, so when we made our attack against the Compact, he was certain to understand everything being said and be able to "cogently give advice."

And, most importantly, to be our witness against the Compact.

As time went on, I did see his language skills improve, fewer thesaurus-type words and more colloquial sayings entering his dialogues and written work. But as to his learning—and believing—our social milieu, that came more slowly.

A part of my mind wondered if he said nothing about our loss, because he did not see our balloons as adding much to the confrontation with the Compact aliens. As if we weren't going to account for much.

Or else—perhaps—he was confident we would replace our losses in time.

The Compact aliens, at least some of them, had set up an illegal base on the Preserve, the island continent opposite the supercontinent we Humans live on. Our supercontinent is simply called Azureign, like our planet. The Preserve had been among the things we colonists were ordered to leave untouched, which we had dutifully done.

So instead, the aliens had used it.

They had broken their own rules, and built a complex of buildings there, destroying all the pristine forest and jungle ecologies that had once presumably existed. We did not know; we had never gone there. Whatever had been lost, there was no it back to life. Thus the aliens had broken more than rules.

Reith Koras had been angry when he told my father that. It was one of several reasons this particular group of Ayi was so upset with the other aliens of the Compact, at least the ones here on Azureign.

As one of four alien species set here to watch us, the Ayi were in the minority. But that did not mean they were not powerful, in their own way.

So Reith was sent by his Lady Calindey to observe and learn and presumably to help at some point.

It was easy to ignore him, even while I knew he was watching us.

Two days after the fire, I walked briskly toward the Assembly Room to meet with my parents and their advisors. I was so focused on the papers in my hands and how I intended to respond to them, that I failed to watch my footing.

Of course I tripped, this time over a fold in the Chem-o-color rug. I landed on my knees and palms, burning and scraping both. I rose to my knees quickly and checked to be sure I hadn't added blood to the golden-yellow pattern the rug had been set to. Seeing none, I checked my palms and found just a slight redness from the friction.

One of the guards had seen the whole thing. However ridiculous I must have appeared, the guard kept a straight face as he put a big battle-trained hand beneath my elbow to lift and guide me on my way.

My awkwardness forever frustrates me. Especially since Zola never has trouble focusing on more than one thing at a time. She astonishes me with her mental juggling. She multi-tasks even more than our formidable mother can.

Here I am, the Le'ul—Crown Prince—and I look like a feeble-minded *querfufu*. My father has patience for me, but Mother just bows her head to hide her expression—usually embarrassment, but sometimes outright anger.

Whether this anger was directed at me and my flaws, or at herself for having borne me, I could not say. Of course her anger at my little brother Kiké is even worse, but Kiké isn't expected to rule. I am.

And Kiké certainly cannot help who he is, whereas we all believe I could be better.

While I knew my own inevitable embarrassed flush was mostly hidden by the darkness of my skin, I still paused to recompose myself before I entered the Assembly Room.

My father's velvet voice said, "Ah here he is," adding a chuckle as I seated myself in the only empty chair. Of course, the day I was late, was the singular day Chondu, the Minister for Education—perpetually late—was on time. My sigh was quiet, but Mother still gave me a sharp look.

I'm sure *she* would have preferred Zola to be Le'ul. Eze and Zeen's sons were both apparent weaklings, to her everlasting shame.

Kezar, Eze of Tehassa, then raised the same papers I had been studying, and read aloud:

15

"'Declaration of Independence,'" he said, "which is independence from the 'Rules of Settlement' and other documents and regulations of the Compact, by *all the citizens of Azureign.*

"Well," he cleared his throat, "I hope we have all had time to read the full document as drafted by the Priestesses at Ysen, and by various national leaders across Azureign. The question before us, given the wording here versus our previous discussions, is this: does Tehassa intend to sign this Declaration and actively participate in the war, or not?"

A fairly long silence fell on the room as various people considered the Eze's words. I was surprised that this had come up for vote *again.* Hadn't we already given our support to this international revolt?

Even Lynly, with its staid Hispanic conservatives, had agreed to send fighters and had contributed significant ships and funds.

A season ago, Zola and I had watched the Dolphinfolk pageant. I had been stunned by the complexity of their history and feelings about their place on Azureign. I know enough of their language to speak with a few individuals, but this—this had shown another complete dimension of their beliefs, and their anger.

The Folk demonstrated their despair at the Compact's rules that had basically enslaved them as Helpers to the "Dirt People," which is to say, *us.* Their growing determination to revolt against their enslavement—and thus against the Compact—had led to this rebellion. How could we not support them?

The balloons that had been burned had been meant to be part of Tehassa's contribution of fighters and materials. The Eze planned five hundred fighting persons to staff the 200 or so balloons we were to send. We also will provide as many ocean-going ships as we can to support the Dolphinfolk and whales of Azureign in their planned attack on the Preserve.

The Folk had also asked for us to provide a contingent of our balloons and people to disable and/or distract the Oracle. This is the Compact aliens' watchpost. This is where the Mengsee, Toridani, and Simbara, along with the minority Ayi, had been posted.

I'm not sure if the Ayi even provide personnel to the Oracle any more, since they are almost as angry as the Folk are.

The Dolphinfolk know that alien "sky-beepers" watch everywhere on the planet. Somehow they can sense them, even though we cannot see them, even with a decent telescope. They are somewhere in our skies, above or perhaps within the Rings. They do not belong to the Ayi.

"How can we back out of the rebellion now, without losing our honor?" Mother asked, bringing me back to the conference table. She voiced my thoughts exactly. "Of course we will sign!"

Most of the Ministers around the table nodded in agreement. My parents were both quick to notice those that didn't, though: Nneka Salisu, who always voted no on anything that would cost money because he saw his job as Minister of the Treasury to allow no one ever to spend any of our funds. Wars are expensive, as he showed with very, *very* old historical documents. Everyone knew what his stance would be, but the Eze had final say in spending our money, despite Salisu's objections.

Also not agreeing, but abstaining by withholding his vote altogether, was Juwon Yahaya, our Minister of Agriculture. He refused his support, because he did not feel we had the right to claim "eminent domain" over animals owned by our Tehassan farmers.

"If they volunteer to donate their horses or oxen or cattle to help or to feed our soldiers or Dragonrider's dragons, that is fine. But I will not seize the fruits of their labor, and I do not think our government should be seen to do so, no matter how valid the purpose."

That had been his stance since the beginning. I believed he did not object to the war for independence *itself*; what he objected to was how we accomplished that rebellion. He would not agree to strip "his" farmers of their crops and herds.

"We will pay for what we use," the Eze said, giving Yahaya a flat stare. "Though we may not be able to afford market price for it all."

Yahaya's mouth opened, but I cut him off.

"After the revolt frees us from Compact limitations," I said as boldly as I could, "everyone's status will improve. The farmers will be compensated in many ways." I saw Zola and my mother nod. I went on, "I do not think our farmers will begrudge us an ox or two if it means they can have modern equipment to plow their fields next year, instead of using those oxen."

"Yes," Zola put in. "Everyone will be free of the restrictions, not just the Dolphinfolk! We will build powerful ships to sail our oceans without Folk help. Everyone, farmers and citymen and all will have access to much better medicine! This *will* benefit all."

"But it is a risk, and I do not vote for risks," Yahaya said.

My father nodded. "I understand what you say, but still, we have five votes for yes, one abstention, and one vote for no," he said.

"So be it," said Zeen Zohari. The Eze's consort, she would be called Queen in other nations. Mother leaned forward, dominating the table. "We sign it now," she said. "And no more of this re-considering over and over! No more going back on our word!"

18

None of the council members even looked at Eze Kezar before nodding agreement. I wondered again how many of them felt my mother was the true ruler of our kingdom.

Zola and I and Kiké, our little brother, have discussed this several times in the past.

Our father is perhaps too kind. He is perhaps not decisive enough. Kiké wonders also if our father is not as smart as our mother.

This felt like a terrible misapprehension, to judge our father and ruler weak, or a fool. But if he knew our opinion, his very laudable kindness meant he would only applaud us for having an opinion, even if it was not flattering to him.

I thought about his remark later and remembered various discussions and circumstances where the Eze let his wife take the lead.

This all did make me wonder what our father really did think. Was it trust in his family that permitted him to defer to her?

Was I being just like him when I let Zola take the lead? Was that a bad thing?

Chapter Two: Poison Pen Letters

Having signed the papers, the Eze ordered Nneka Salisu to buy silk from wherever it could be found, and to hire extra sewing experts to join those silks into replacement envelopes.

We only have about ninety balloons right now, counting everything, including those that deliver mail and supplies around the islands. However desperate we might be to provide the balloons we'd promised to the rebellion forces, we would not strip our isles of those services. It took about a dozen, plus their crews, to maintain the cycle of deployment, flowing with the winds. Usually this included a stop somewhere in Lynly and occasionally on our mainland peninsula to the southwest. These rotations are important to the health and morale of our nation.

I'd made the trip several times, at first to learn exactly what they did for our people, and later because I loved the experience. You can see almost our entire nation from a balloon. Including the Falls. Mist and roiling water accompanied the deposit of all that water into the Azure Ocean, making the view mysterious and beautiful.

Eventually the Inner Sea will come to some equilibrium, where it shrinks enough that the water level will fall below the edges of the Falls. While many rivers across the supercontinent empty into the Inner Sea, the total volume of water it gains is still less than it loses over the Falls. During the millennium Humans had been on Azureign, we had seen the water level fall. A portion of the Inner Sea, now called the Swampen Sea, used to be meters deep. Now it was almost too shallow for boats. Light skiffs could cross the western end, and only shallow draft tugs and barges could make it through the neck to Avordan Town.

That is a place I would like to see. Perhaps one day I could take a balloon or a boat all the way around the Inner and Swampen Seas.

Our planet is gorgeous. I yearn to see more of it.

My father the Eze ordered a small formal dinner to celebrate Kiké's Name Day. All of my littlest brother's favorite foods were on the menu, and his few friends and favorite relatives were seated around the table.

Treats for Kiké included the rare and exotic *pineapple* and the tree-fruit called *cherries*, which for some reason have a hard time growing on Azureign. We had reference books that showed these two were common on Earth, but the unknown gods of the Universe made them quite picky here on Azureign, and we do not have the tech or the knowledge to fix them.

These imported fancy foods are the reason we were at first misled as to what poisoned my father...but no one else.

With my friend Tengda La!ima's help, I led the group that inspected the foods, the wine only he drank, even the coffee served with dessert. We tested with every test we have, but could find nothing.

But I go ahead of myself; first, what happened:

Kiké's Name Day dinner began well, each of us congratulating Kiké and giving him a small handmade gift. I had built a lapstand to hold a book, so that he could more easily read in bed. It would replace the one I'd made a dozen years before, when my skill was smaller. The years and the flaws were finally adding together to make the old one collapse.

The new one was made from feurla wood I'd cut to shape, fitted together, and polished to a deep reddish-gold sheen. He seemed pleased with it.

Tengda gave him a platter of baklava she had made. The crispy layers, slathered in honey and crumbled nuts, made him grin in anticipation.

I caught her eye and mouthed, "Thank you," which made her smile and blush.

Kiké's legs had never developed well, so he was bedridden for much of the time. Today, many of his other gifts also accommodated this disability along with his love of reading.

He is able to sit or lie down, but standing or walking any distance is difficult, painful and slow.

He'd been cheated of any chance to play like the other children, royal or otherwise.

Father's gift addressed this particular limitation. It was a handmade wheelchair, one that could be adapted to many circumstances outdoors, with big plass wheels and fat rubber tires, so Kiké could play certain games both indoors and out. He could throw and catch and move across a court in this chair. I think Father was hoping he would use it to get outside more.

Mostly, Kiké sits and reads in his room. He can, with the help of his arm-braces, move three or four steps on his own. Thus, his suite is filled with various chairs, couches and benches so he can change position. The bathroom has a tub he can slide into and pull himself out of. His arms are very strong.

His sitting room has the most windows of all the suites in the palace, being set in a turret with almost 270 degrees of glass panels so he can look outdoors, or open the French door section and let in the water-laden breezes of our home. His view includes a portion of the falls beside our capitol, Montmarras. He can also see the hedge maze on the palace grounds, and part of the city market, the stalls and carts dwindling with distance down the hill to Montmarras valley, and ultimately, the cascade section of the Falls far below.

Father loves creating celebrations that especially include my little brother. That night, as we ate our dessert—ginger-filled Naming Day cookies—and drank our coffee, we were entertained by zookeepers.

These well-trained people brought out various wild animals and demonstrated their natural abilities, which seemed to delight Kiké, even though he is now perhaps too old for such antics, at fourteen Azureign years.

Once, the lands that now made up Tehassa had been bigger. The rocks and ice chunks dropped onto Azureign's surface during terraforming had changed things...to make the planet more livable, supposedly.

From that bombardment, though, we had consequences such as lively tectonics, including volcanoes, earthquakes and the cracks across the lands that became Tehassa—a broken chain of islands where once had stood a low mountain range holding back the Inner Sea. Instead, we now have the spectacular but impassable Falls at the Edge of the World, and Tehassa has less land mass than any other nation of our world. Which is why we became adept at ballooning, to cross the Falls, to make use of every hectare of our islands.

Later, all colonies settled from Earth brought fertilized embryos of the most endangered Terran animals.

Some had no doubt recovered on Earth, like a special species called Sumatran tiger. The Library of Humanity had told us these now (well, *then,* meaning a millennia ago) flourished in its homelands. Some declining beasts on Earth also had been replenished by animals that had flourished on colonial worlds.

Their addition back into the gene pool meant much more robust populations.

We on Azureign had been given a variety of big cats. First-in settlers had hand-raised and released two types of tigers, and snow leopards, in the Queensland and Ba Mi mountains. Also cheetahs on the plains of Kendai and Lhasa, and small fishing cats in the forests of north Lynly and Queensland. Our zoo here on Montmarras trades with zoos in Vai Tilden, and other areas of Azureign, to ensure strong cross-breeding. We also take in occasional orphaned wild cubs.

So our keeper and his friend (from the nation that was formerly called Maladh) brought out various cats and showed some of their natural behaviors—though of course our Small Hall was much too short to show off the cheetah's splendid running speed, for example. Instead, they showed videos of the animals sprinting across the plains of Kendai, chasing their natural prey: Thompson's gazelles, which had also been among the colonial seed and gamete banks.

Kiké was particularly entranced by the tree-climbing antics of the little spotted fishing cat, who coolly demonstrated his ability to flip a fish out of a tank of water. And eat it.

Kiké laughed out loud. "I hope that didn't spoil anyone's desire for dessert!" he said.

I remember my father had smiled broadly at that, glad he had been able to charm his youngest son.

It was not until late that night that we knew something had poisoned the Eze.

I was alerted by many footsteps in the hallway outside my door, and alarmed voices raised in my parents' quarters. I stumbled to their doorway—both big doors standing wide open—and stood in confusion, dressed only in my pajama bottoms.

The palace doctor was here, and a nurse, both doing medical things to my father. My mother, in her dressing gown, was shooing ministers and distant relatives away from my father's bedside.

"Give him room to breathe!" She yelled, finally exasperated by their stupid fascination.

I finished what she'd begun by shooing everyone not-family outside into the hall where they moved to form clumps of whispering folk down the length of the corridor.

My friend Tengda showed up in her leopard-spotted-cloth robe, a reminder of the evening's earlier pleasant activities. She drifted closer to me and took my hand. I nodded to her but returned my attention to my father.

My sister, seated beside our father on the bed, held his hand. I remained at the doorway, appointing myself guardian of his space, and watching and listening to what the doctor said.

I was still standing there at the doorway when the convulsions began.

"Definitely poison," the doctor murmured. "But I don't recognize it; I cannot guess what it is at all."

My sister suggested something I could not hear, but the doctor shook his head, cradling my father's head and lifting him to a half-sitting position. This did nothing to stop the convulsions, but did seem to ease the Eze's breathing.

Three more sequences of spasms and gasping breaths, and then...my father the Eze was gone. His hand fell loose from my sister's, his breath and all movement stopped. I stepped into the room, gaze frozen upon the lifeless form on the bed, my chest and arms going numb as my mind understood. The Eze was dead.

The doctor wiped a white substance from Father's lips after collecting a sample in a small glass jar. Then he closed my father's eyes after peering closely at each of those eyes, a magnifying glass held up by the nurse to assist him.

Tight-lipped, he stepped back and shook his head.

"I am so sorry, but without knowing the specific chemical, there was nothing I could do."

Zohari, my mother, keened and ululated the rest of the night. My sister Zola joined her from time to time as did some of the women who had served with the Eze for many years, including my friend Tengda. Their little cluster of hugging, crying, hand-squeezing women had no place for a male, the son of the Eze or not.

I walked to the bed and helped the nurse place the ritual covering over my father's body, so he was draped in heavy embroidered silk from the neck down. We folded his hands together across his lower chest, and then placed his simplest gold crown on his head atop his still-thick black curls.

All this while my mother continued to vocally grieve, my sister and my friend holding her hands to keep her from scratching herself.

My brother arrived, propped into his littlest rolling chair. He looked to me for an explanation, but I had nothing to tell him. Not at that time. I signaled him to roll back out into the hall and joined him there.

"The doctor is still studying it," I said, once he might hear me above the wailing.

Face wet with tears, he sobbed until he became frantic, almost hysterical, and I asked his guardian to return him to his room. "A gentle sedative might calm him; perhaps in some tea."

The man nodded, eyes sad, and rolled him away.

I mourned the Eze, quietly, steadily, knowing his goodness was now gone from this place.

My father may not have been any kind of genius in thought, but his deeds were kind, his persona gentle, and I had to wonder, over and over in my head like the refrain of a clever song: Who could have done this to him? And *why?*

Zola and Kiké and I had our own private discussion, exploring how the poison—whatever it was—had been introduced.

The physician had been appalled at his failure to even identify it, much less suggest its source. Every food and drink was tested, as far as our limited chemistry allowed.

Besides, everything that had been served had been eaten by at least one other person, and no one else had been the least bit ill. Only the wine the Eze had chosen for himself had been consumed by him exclusively. And that we tested over and over, with no result.

"Something could have been added to the cup when the wine was served," Kiké suggested.

"Or anything else that was served to Father," Zola said. "His plate, his silverware, his napkin."

"That is all being examined and tested," I said, feeling like we'd said all this before. We just kept going over the same things, *ad infinitum.* "I think we should look in his office and the desk he uses in their bedroom."

Zola looked at me and blinked. Her perfect cocoa-colored skin glowed like satin, her dark brown and tilted eyes a gift from our mother that neither I nor my brother had gotten.

Instead, Father's golden-brown hazel eyes, set deep beneath our foreheads and heavy brows, looked back at her. Our lashes are thick and considered desirable, which irked Zola, as hers were not. But she did not really begrudge us our one claim to handsomeness.

We all knew any lovers or spouses either of us sons managed to attract weren't going to be ours because of our looks. But even Kiké had access to money and power that were a strong draw to certain ladies. Unfortunately, these tended to be ladies neither of us found attractive in return.

Now that Father the Eze was dead, I would be crowned and must be promptly wed to ensure our line continued. A prospect I did not look forward to, being married to one of the silly court girls or a foreign lady whose customs I would not know at all.

But as it turned out, I was putting the cart before the horse.

Instead of seeing me crowned, as would have been proper, Mother seized the reins and took over control of Tehassa.

I managed to have free time for a couple hours while my mother was engaged elsewhere. I went into their suite and strode directly to the Eze's desk. This was not considered his office, it was simply a place he often worked, where he had privacy and quiet unlike his "working" office, downstairs.

Here I found some personal correspondence he'd had with his friend in Lhasa, and also another friend, a researcher in northern Lynly.

Among the other things on the desktop were a few news-scrolls. These are our substitute for a newspaper like many other nations have. The scrolls are a weekly summary put together by the Eze's news agency (also known as spies) that had personnel in the field both locally and elsewhere.

Spies, or news gatherers, they are people who work with and listen to common citizens, foreign citizens and foreign courts or councils. Along with these sources are a few higher-ranked people who check out things like new findings from the Library of Humanity and the Priestess towers at Ysen.

All this information is collated, curated and then published and distributed to all our people from the Eze to the farmer's hall in the tiny town of Abia on the Inner Island chain.

So I glanced through these, but saw nothing my father had marked for attention.

Then, buried beneath this pile of news-scrolls, I found something far more concerning.

Someone, or several people as I discovered with close reading, had been sending the Eze threatening letters. They claimed there would be "serious consequences" if he continued his policy of joining the revolt against the Compact.

Again, these people ignored the fact that the war would carry on *whether our nation participated in it or not.* Their claims that the Eze was risking our right to live on Azureign was completely bogus because of that one fact alone.

In any event, we plan to sidestep that rule with our very strong claim that the Compact rules had *already been broken*—by the aliens.

I redirected my focus from that frustration to my purpose here and now: I was looking for exactly why, and possibly how, my father had been killed.

The nasty letters were a strong clue. I collected them all together, then counted them. All told, there were eight letters with outright threats, along with several more vaguely threatening but highly critical ones.

From the handwriting, I could see there were at least two different senders, maybe more. A couple, dated earliest, were more general threats. The later ones became much more specific and dire.

For example, one stated: "No Eze! One vote per person, one nation!" and went on to promise after the overthrow of the monarchy, the protestors would establish a democracy!

Here they completely forgot history.

Tehassa had once tried to create a democratic state. One simple fact eluded these protestors, just as the democracy had eluded us: It was extremely difficult to discuss or vote on anything when communications between even the nearest islands took days, and the furthest ones and the mainland contacts sometimes took tendays, each way.

Discussions around each issue took seasons, decisions even longer. The nation was paralyzed to make a decision during that time. Power had to be more centrally located simply for logistical reasons.

Humanity is odd. Each of our little herds or prides clearly wants leadership. We are willing to accept a single leader who is essentially a king or a President, with supreme power.

But then at the same time, we can be extremely unwilling to trust a democratically elected local power, squabbling endlessly over this or that aspect of the elected representative's decisions.

On the one hand, we'd accept an inherited supreme leader, on the other, we didn't trust an elected one. It was a paradox everyone seemed to ignore.

In fact, even our alien Ayi observer found nothing unusual about our systems of government here on Azureign. Or at least he hadn't said so, among the many other things he hadn't said.

The letter I ended up showing to my siblings was the worst—the most threatening and specific. Written in red ink (which is difficult but possible to make, from various herbs, saps and tree barks), it clearly stated the Eze would be poisoned.

"I don't suppose they were foolish enough to tell us what he'd be poisoned *with?*" Kiké grumbled.

I gave him a grim smile, and kept reading aloud: "By this, my very hand, will he die," I read out.

Then abruptly Zola yelped and snatched the pages from my hands.

"Go!" she shouted, "Wash your hands, wash your face. Change your clothes!" I stared at her a moment, shocked, and she waved me on with one hand, while with the other, she threw the papers into the fireplace and stirred the coals alive to consume them.

"What?" Kiké asked as I finally realized the same thing Zola had: the *pages themselve*s were poisonous! The ink, or the paper, I didn't know, but I'd touched them both.

I rushed to the sink, and using fresh running water pumped from the Inner Sea and the flakes of handmade soap that sat in the bin beside the basin, I scrubbed. Washed, rinsed, washed again, including my face. Then I stripped off all but my underclothes. I used a pillowcase from Father's bedside to stuff the clothes into, then washed hands and face again, adding the towel to the presumably-contaminated clothes and linens.

"Those should be burned," Zola said. "Wash again."

"We can't be certain it's water soluble," I said, using a fluffy brushed linen towel to dry myself off.

"No, but it's likely," my sister said, while she washed her own hands. "Whether the paper is coated, or if it was the ink, it still needed to be easily transferrable to the reader in order to do its work."

"The reader" being my father. And now possibly, us.

"That means it had to be soluble in something," Kiké put in, understanding and sharing our realization of the poisoning agent.

"Oh, godlings in the skies," Zola said, eyes wide. "They really *were* poison pen letters."

None of us thought that was the least bit funny, but I could imagine the cruel face of the poisoner, finding the irony delicious.

Kiké again spoke, looking at the fire that had consumed the letters. "Now we can't figure out who sent what."

"No. But perhaps having succeeded in murdering our Father—"

"The Eze!" Zola put in.

I finished, "—we will hear the spiteful creature crowing among the crowds." I chewed my lip, thinking. "Or, possibly by his or her own death, if they weren't careful enough when applying the poison."

Zola nodded.

"On my Name Day!" Kiké burst into tears. Zola and I both moved to his chair and bent to hug him. Really, we were helpless to offer him the comfort he needed.

And in the same way, there was nothing we could do to change what had happened to the Eze.

But we could certainly find out who had been responsible.

Chapter Three: Dissent

Before our Eze's death was even announced to all our people, our mother, the Zeen, seized control of our government in Montmarras. She told me privately that once she found the assassin she intended to step down and elevate me, as was proper.

Thus, she ignored traditional protocol, which would have been to see me crowned Eze as soon as the mourning period for my father was over. She felt finding the Eze's murderers would help reassure our people that our family was firmly in control, that the government was in no danger of falling.

She did begin questioning immediately the servitors in the palace who had delivered the mail.

The picture she discovered wasn't pretty. Over several years, various servitors in the mail room had one by one been replaced. Of the eight people who worked there now, only one was affiliated with a friendly house, and had been there for years. The others were new and careful placements.

From this, we learned two things: First, and most notably, this usurpation or rebellion within Farnesse had begun well before even the idea of a break with the Compact had been planned. Therefore, their bellowings about the dangers of breaking with the Compact aliens were just noise. They'd intended this rebellion all along, for other reasons. The rebellion just gave them a more obvious excuse.

And second, we learned that our enemy lay within either Corrigan or Lawal, or both.

We've never had a good relationship with Corrigan, but Lawal was a surprise. Their family runs Isubu Omi, the island between Montmarras and Mers. They've always seemed middle-of-the-road as far as their political affiliations and progressiveness were concerned.

Lawal's isle was by no means one of the more powerful or wealthy—up until recently. Their new mulberry orchards had begun to flourish, and as their trees grew, their silk production grew, and their wealth along with it. We had ordered thousands of meters of silk for the balloons intended to join the attack on the Oracle and Preserve. They had produced them without objection, raking in the monies the crown sent them and dutifully producing meters of silk.

And all the while they'd *perhaps* been plotting behind our backs.

They'd placed two of their people in our mail room...and as it turned out, elsewhere in our house as well.

We had underestimated them.

My mother, the Zeen, ordered Achojah Lawal, the Governor of Isubu Omi, and Tarrah Corrigan, current Governor of Barque, into her presence.

For this formal hearing, she asked for me by her side—to add to her legitimacy, I suppose. As if she was Regent for me, because we all knew I should be crowned.

She counts me a weakling, or a child, that she doesn't allow me to deal with these families on my own. Instead, everything is under her...I want to say *control,* but I suppose she sees it as *strong leadership.*

I was only *allowed* to stand beside her—and watch—while these powerful family representatives come before us.

I begin to wonder when I shall be Eze, not that I was ever eager to accept that role.

Tarrah Corrigan has the violent red hair of her forebears, which she has grown in a curly blanket to her waist. Even as old as she is, she leaves it loose, as if she was an unwed maiden.

Her robes and legwraps are blood red and black.

Her son, Jereth, stands beside her. Both of them wear expressions and body stances of strength and defiance. Jereth is dressed more modestly, his robes a mild green and gold, making him pale beside his mother.

Achojah Lawal stands by himself, representing his family without anyone at his side. His stance was arrogant, as we have come to expect from Lawal. But until now, they have been relatively neutral and cooperative. His robes, at least, were the white of contrition, of peace-making, in a style I had not seen before.

"Where is the Eze?" Tarrah Corrigan said, making a show of looking around the room. Her stiff flat collar of wire-strung glass beads—meant to imitate an unwed Maasai woman's—which she is neither: not unwed, not Maasai. She is a woman, and I am sure she intended to show strength, but it gave her instead the aura of a child playing dress-up.

Worse, she had not woven in any white beads, the color of peace and purity. Most of hers were red, with black and green highlights.

Beads and clothing of these colors have ancient meanings, but they have come and stayed with us since we left Earth, so long ago:

Red means warriors, blood, bravery.

Black means the people and their struggles.

Green stands for the land, the portions they own and protect and nurture.

Tarrah Corrigan included no blue beads, for energy and water. Also the stiff collar lacked yellow and orange, meaning she had no intentions of fair dealing or compromising her position. Nor was there a speck of the white of peace anywhere in her clothing or adornments.

"I will speak with no one less than the Eze," she said, trying to stare down the Zeen.

Achojah Lawal glanced at her with amusement in his gaze. He may have felt the same way I did, that she did herself no favors in her dress or words: she was more like an angry child, stamping her foot.

"That is my question as well," my mother said in her low hoarse voice. "*Where is the Eze?*" Her granite brown eyes moved from the woman in the overwrought costume to meet Lawal's steady gaze.

"I have heard he has been murdered," Lawal said in a likewise steady voice.

"Ah," the Zeen said. "But murdered by whom?" She leaned back in her chair—not the Eze's chair, but her own, made likewise from ebony wood from Earth, but less ornate than the Eze's—where I was not yet allowed to sit. It was empty but for one of the Eze's crowns resting on the woven jacquard-covered seat.

At a signal from my mother, Zola entered the room. She carried on a wooden tray, a bottle of red ink and a stack of handmade papers, like those the letters had been written on.

Our alchemists were still testing the red ink and papers to find out which had carried the poison, but my mother had made up her mind that it didn't matter which: they had been used to poison her husband.

She would find their source.

What the Zeen hoped to see here, I'm fairly certain, was what reaction our two suspects might show at our display on Zola's tray. Could we provoke a guilty response?

As I had supposed, Lawal merely seemed interested, eyeing the items on the tray with curiosity. Puzzlement made his forehead wrinkle.

36

But the Corrigan had a much different reaction. She paled and frowned, glancing at Zola's face, then mine, then my mother's. By now my sister and I were almost as good at the granite-eyed stare of the Zeen as she was herself, so Tarrah Corrigan did not learn anything from us cubs.

She looked back at the ink and paper, her gaze resting longest on the bottle of red ink.

Her face became so pale her skin was almost gray. I have to say, this combination of gray face, bright red hair, the bright colors of her costume, gave her the appearance of an ill or dying jester, like we sometimes invite to give entertainment (though in good health, of course). Explosive colors, face paint, humorous antics and words. Though she was none of those.

Her son, Jereth, stepped forward, reaching out a hand toward the items on the tray.

I met my mother's gaze. The Zeen's expression bore her fiercest lioness aspect: She would attack soon. Not yet.

We saw that clearly the son had not been involved. What Zola carried were *not* the actual ingredients we had found in the home of one of the new mail workers. They were just made to look like those things.

But Jereth did not know that.

"Jereth!" his mother called before he could touch what she clearly believed was the poison ink. He jerked his hand back and turned to look at his mother, eyebrows raised.

"Thank you for demonstrating our enemy, Jereth Corrigan," the Zeen of Tehassa said, claws out, teeth bared. "You, dear, will remain at our court until such time as we believe it is safe to return you to your isle."

Then she glared at Jereth's mother, shifting her bulk forward so she loomed over the thin woman.

"You, Tarrah Corrigan, are accused. The remainder of your family are banished from Montmarras for the foreseeable future. Barque loses its vote in council and will pay extreme reparations.

"*You* will remain imprisoned here until you are called for trial for the murder of the Eze."

"I did no such thing!" she protested. "There are others who engage in such interference. Others have murdered him!" I could see her gulp. Desperate, she claimed: "I was forced to help them!"

A pair of our husky guards approached and again like a child, the Corrigan woman shamed herself struggling against them.

Experienced with such things, the guards each grasped one of her upper arms and simply lifted her off her feet and carried her away, still kicking. So swiftly was she removed from the court of the ruling family that if not for Jereth, we might never have known she was there.

We who mourned our Eze.

The Zeen glanced at a second pair of guards that stood by the side entrance to our hearing room. "Take all the mailroom workers but the Dabada clan man to the city cells to await trial." These were all the new people in the mail room.

The single Dabada family worker she clearly thought was still loyal, though I was not at all sure that was the case. The man had been in charge of the others; how could he have been innocent if he personally oversaw the internal workings of that room each day? The workings that had included delivery of the poisoned letters.

"I will consider whether Corrigan will be stripped of your holdings on Barque and your other isles," Mother said to Jereth Corrigan. "You will attend council without a vote until such time as we understand the depth of your family's betrayal."

His mouth a straight line, his eyes half-lidded in either shame or contrivance—or possibly acceptance, I could not tell. He nodded acquiescence, though, then gave me an eyes wide open glance before turning and walking away with our house guards leading him. He'd be under house arrest, our guards surrounding his quarters.

When he had left the room, Zola set the tray down on the table beside me and plopped herself on her empty chair there. "He loves you, you know," she murmured to me.

"Who? *Jereth?*"

She smirked, pleased with herself for yet again noticing something I had not. She nodded, then noticed the Zeen was eyeing us both, eyebrow raised.

"Is this mutual?" she asked me.

I shook my head. "I had not even realized," I answered her as honestly as I knew how. I suppose it was a little flattering that I held even an enemy's love, though I'd been unaware of it.

My mother's face folded into a hard scowl. "You are so oblivious," she said. "The same as with Tengda."

Tengda La!lima, my friend of many years, she meant.

Yes, I had only recently noticed her adoration, which, I'd been told, had gone on for as long as we'd known each other. My sister and mother both had been exasperated to have to tell me what they expected me to have known already.

"You could do worse than Tengda," Zola had said. She'd been suggesting I should marry the La!lima woman.

I sighed. Tengda was a friend. I did not think of her as a *wife.*

Now Zohari Kell, my mother, took a deep breath and shook her head. "I will make this a requirement of your elevation to Eze, Zeden: you must have a spouse before you are crowned. It would be good if we had an heir on the way, as well."

I scowled at the polished wood tray, then glanced at my sister, avoiding my mother's gaze. Zola was still studying our mother's face, perhaps to learn whether that was the only reason I had not already been crowned.

Then the Ayi youth who had been standing invisibly against the far wall, observing as usual, nodded to me and my mother and exited the room without a word.

Probably to report to his Lady, Calindey, who was *somewhere,* aboard her ship.

Our meeting broke up with me still thinking about marriage.

Many Eze had risen to the throne of Tehassa without meeting that requirement. Instead they'd married long afterward, with no heir in sight.

I begrudgingly had to agree that it was perhaps wise for *this* Ras Le'ul to do so, given the unrest in our nation. Without a clear heir, the people of Tehassa would be even more uncomfortable than they seemed to be now.

Most were not willing to see Kiké on the throne, given his ill-formed body. They wanted a leader who was majestic and strong. Not that I am, particularly, but I *am* the Ras Le'ul. The people know I am legitimate. They are aware that I am clever, and a decent enough fighter to lead my scouts and spies. I can probably pretend majesty well enough, if I put my mind to it. I am *acceptable.*

I knew Zola would be good, but our people do not like change any more than any other Human tribe does: there hadn't been a female Eze for over four hundred years. They'd rather not break that tradition.

So I considered Jereth. If I made such a match, we would need also to add a woman to bear my heirs. I shook my internal head; even for that, or perhaps *especially* for that, Tengda was still wrong. I could not do that to my friend. I would need to look for someone else.

I like Jereth well enough. We'd fostered together at my uncle's home on Mers for several years. And I know that marriage to a Corrigan would have strong benefits for our nation—if nothing else it should shut up all those who felt Corrigan leadership would make a good change.

With him by my side, we would have Corrigan strength alongside stolid K!elli! traditions. I wasn't drawn to the idea of Jereth even so much as I was toward Tengda, though, so that was a problem. Such a match should make our people happy, however unpleasant it might be for the Eze, who would be me.

Still, Tengda.

I did talk to her. The first thing I did was apologize for not returning her love.

"You have always been my friend, Tengda."

She smiled her shy smile at me.

Tengda La!lima, like many of the women of Tehassa, is curvy and soft. Beneath that surface softness, I know there is the strength of great fortitude. Not traditionally beautiful, she was saved from plainness by her lovely eyes and smile.

I did have the irreverent thought that if she bore Tehassa's heirs, the children would have a guarantee of stunning eyes. Between my lashes and her own deeply tilted eyes with their clear dark gold irises, any such heir's gaze would be mesmerizing.

But I felt I'd betrayed my friend, even thinking that thought. Genetics was even less a reason to marry than friendship, or so it seems to me.

Tengda, always kind, responded, "I am glad to be your friend, Zeden. You have always been welcome to confide in me, if you have need to talk to someone."

I nodded, already knowing that.

41

Marriage? I gazed at her, trying that on in my mind, but I just...could not make the idea work. To wed my friend would break our friendship, I was certain. And that was too precious to me to risk.

Later that tenday, we learned that there had been an attack on our ancestral home as well as the murder of our Eze: our K!elli! manor house overlooking the south Falls on Mers was overrun by protestors.

These attackers managed, in the confusion, to pull my Uncle Igbo and his eldest son out of the manor house and throw them over the falls. The son might survive, but they'd already found my uncle's broken body, pushed to shore by the ocean waves far below.

I mourned his loss. I'd fostered there in my early teen years and had become close to the jolly older man. His son and I never got along, but I still learned of his injuries and possible death with sadness.

Less important, but still a sign of their temporary insanity, the demonstrators destroyed ages-old murals inside the house and burned many of the furnishings in a fire in the courtyard, which spread to the stables and other outbuildings. Our family's base on Mers was mostly destroyed. Many of our historical links to our distant past on Earth had been lost along with it.

During their mad destruction, these rioters managed to kill several of our loyal servitors—people who had never lifted a weapon in their lives. They were murdered simply for being there.

What had these idiots hoped to gain from this?

The people who had done this had misconstrued the power structure within the palace, and especially had underestimated how strongly we would react.

They threatened our way of life. They destroyed our ancestral home. Some of them had murdered the Eze—who knew how many were linked to Corrigan?

We could never let this stand. *I* wouldn't.

Though I did not yet have the authority to do so, I sent two hundred of our trained military men to Mers to clear out the rebels.

I wished I could go personally to suppress this rebellion, but I needed to maintain the (future) Eze's royal presence in Montmarras to reassure our people.

Between my uncle's remaining guardsmen and this powerful group of two hundred I sent, they caught the perpetrators. They tried and executed six men and one woman who had instigated the riot that had gone much too far. The Captain reported to me that most of the seven had remained unrepentant even at the end, though two of them, a man and the woman, had expressed sorrow and regret.

They were executed regardless, and in front of the villagers and farmers of the region.

Chastened, the people returned to their own nearby businesses and farms.

I ordered the families of the executed trouble-makers to rebuild our family home, using their own funds for supplies, and their own people for the labor.

I knew their peaceful neighbors must look at them askance. What had provoked them so against us?

How had they goaded themselves into such actions?

I felt I had made a sufficient response to their families' betrayals, whatever their reasoning. I also hoped keeping them busy with the rebuild meant they had no energy for further displays against our leadership.

I left two dozen extra guards and recalled the rest back to Montmarras.

There was nothing we could do about the destroyed priceless tapestries and other furnishings, nor our dead household staff, but mourn them. Nothing could bring them back.

I mourned my father's death far more profoundly than the loss of those people and especially those *things*. But I had to continue to wonder what on Azureign the murderers and destroyers thought to gain by their destructions.

Why assassinate the leader of a peaceful nation?

How did murdering my father help anyone in any way? He had been beloved by his people as much as his family, and I began to believe some outside agency must have provoked the murder and the riot.

Would the aliens of the Compact try to destabilize our nation for some reason incomprehensible to us?

There was scant evidence they'd provoked the coups in Jia and Maladh, which had happened just before whoever-it-was had begun undermining our government in Tehassa. But why do any of this?

I remembered from history lessons from our tutor that some historians believed there were natural cycles to human government, and that when such a cycle came to an end, there would be revolt. Sometimes these would be economic revolutions, sometimes technological, and sometimes global upsets arising from people who were fed up with the *status quo*.

So in sum, I didn't know what to think. We would keep our eyes wide open, and do our best to protect our people.

INTERVAL: Ayi Ships

Here I am telling you the utility of Ayi spaceships, including the large *kej*-ships. (These are town-sized vessels; that is, one large enough, holding a big enough population, that it could be considered a mobile city that *is* a ship.) From *kej*-ships all the way down in size to passenger shuttles and tiny unmanned observation drones, they are used to house Ayi people, work in space, and watch throughout the galaxy, wherever Ayi have interests.

Ayi ships, particularly House Dzarn ships, are differing from other species' spaceships in one distinct way: Ours can randomly access null space. This we call "random jump drive." We create a small pocket universe in which we can hide, rest, make repairs, or make the calculations for jump out (emerging from null) a *long distance away* from the point in "real space" or normal space, where we entered null.

We can thus jump without having to be at a jump point.

We have learned to do this in this way: The Cuy, who are our friends and advisors, and who are the most advanced species of the Compact, are wholly spiritual beings. That is, they have no physical presence that can be touched. They do not need ships to travel the universe. They travel through a "nowhere place" called null space. (We are not certain, but they may live there, too. Such as "living" is for Cuy.)

It was our knowing this about the Cuy that gave Dzarn the impetus to learn all we could about null space and how we might use it ourselves.

All our ships, from largest to smallest, are having equipped a null space access engine. It takes virtually no energy to slip into and out of null.

It takes considerable computing ability, however, to plot emergence points properly when exiting null. Each time we do this (go into null), we create a new pocket universe, or so we think. Then, when we exit, we leave that small space behind, abandoned, but still in existence.

If an error in calculating the coordinates for jump-out from null occurs, it is entirely possible to emerge (or be attempting to emerge) into a large solid object, like a planet, a solar mass or a space station that exists at that point. You might think this would result in instant death, but it does not.

Instead, the ship attempting to exit null is "bounced" back into its pocket universe in null. After correctly re-calculating a different jump-out point, that ship can then still manage to safely emerge. There is no effect upon the solid object in normal space before or after the emergence attempt. This is likely because they exist in two different dimensions, or universes, one of which "refuses" entry to the other, because of our miscalculated coordinates.

In the case of a smaller mass, such as another ship existing at the jump-out point (this happened twice over the last five millennia), the ships will be knocked apart by the emergence of the second ship at that place. This may occur violently enough to have fatal results, or not, depending primarily upon velocity and mass of the two ships (or a small asteroid, for example.) that are involved in the collision.

That is, normal space will "permit" emergence from null at a point, if and only if any mass that exists at that point is small enough. The laws of physics prohibit two objects from existing in the same place at the same time, hence they are thrown apart.

If, for any reason a ship's computers are failing, or the ship is otherwise unable to calculate emergence point coordinates, it can be stuck in null. This can be fatal, if a ship is stuck long enough and life support runs out. For this reason, there are a few "safe points" designated by our people around the galaxy. A lost ship can jump to one of these safe points using pre-calculated & memorized emergence data. From these "safe points," they can call for help using small drones.

Safe points are similar to fixed jump points in that their location is "known" and re-accessible from both null and normal space, and are created using a normal jump drive (not an Ayi random jump drive), so it remains accessible to all who know of it and require its safety.

Also, it is recommended and wise to pre-calculate a desired emergence point *before* even jumping *into* null. Such a pre-set jump route is also quicker to utilize and can often be done by "hand" by a decent navigator in the event of total computer failure.

We are never encountering anyone or anything (not even Cuy) when we access null space via the random jump drive, which we have been doing for the past 5000 years (Earth measurement). The pocket universes created are apparently not adjacent to nor connected to one another in any way. Thus we cannot travel between them, nor can we communicate between them, in null. We must jump back into "normal" space to access communications.

In other words, a flotilla of adjacent ships and/or drones, can access null at the exact same time, starting from right beside one another and they will not ever "see" one another in null because each ship or drone creates its own space. This suggests that each has created its *own new space*—its own pocket universe—within null space.

What this means for travel and logistics, is that we can calculate, jump into null space, calculate, and almost immediately jump out somewhere else. As long as we have accurate location coordinates, this can translate into virtually instantaneous travel across great distances.

However, the catch point is *"accurate location coordinates."* **The farther we try to jump, the more exact the coordinates for emergence need to be.** This puts a limit on how far away the destination for a jump out of null can be, particularly if we are traveling in previously unknown or unmapped space.

Because of this limitation on random null jumps, Ayi ships also each have a jump drive similar to that used by every other known species (including Humanity).

This jump drive system requires *a known jump point with a known destination given by that particular jump point.* That is, *both the jump-in and jump-out points are* fixed *and must be known in order to make a jump.* This limits the places everyone can go. Hence the enormous interest in our random jump drive.

While standard jump drives allow a ship to travel via a form of null space, it does not seem to be the "same" null as Ayi random-jump pocket universes. (Though this is difficult to assess, certain mathematics have ascertained they are unrelated to one another. They are separate dimensions within the known and unknown universes.)

It is the fixed jump points to several early Earth colonies that were lost (that is the location coordinates of the entry/exit points were lost) during a time of upheaval on Earth approximately 600 years ago. This led to several stranded Human colonies, which have all since been found again, with the exception of one, named Sandovar.

For "local" logistics, like helping the Dolphinfolk and colonists of Azureign, using our random null jumps is being simple and helpful. There is no limit on how close to a planetary mass a jump into or out of this null can be made, as long as the calculations are correct.

Even if we have just a single ship or shuttle, we can—almost—be in two places at once. That is, within a relatively small space such as the atmospheric envelope of a planet, the jumps can be so quick as to be indistinguishable from simultaneous.

This is how Calindey originally was planning to help the Dolphinfolk and Human revolt: jumping quickly back and forth between the Preserve and the Oracle sites via null space pocket universes, as needed to help.

However, we may now be joined by other Ayi ships at Azureign. These are other House Dzarn ship owners, or in two cases, other Houses of Ayi, who are finding the Simbara and Mengsee—and possibly also Toridani—actions here to be dismayingly ugly, unexpected, and perverse.

All these Ayi ships will help us protect the colonists, and the unique Helper species Dolphinfolk, as they bring their mighty protests to the attention of the full Compact with this, their revolt.

I am often asked: are our Ayi ships armed?

Every ship of our species carries various armaments, primarily because every ship of all other Compact species carries weapons of some kind, now without exception. Humanity has discovered by tragic means that they cannot explore the galaxy safely without weapons to fight off the more aggressive among the other species, although their unarmed probes were successful for a while.

Despite having armaments, it is difficult for Ayi to *use* weapons against other intelligent species, because of *pejiin*, which I will explain about later.

Note:

My friend Kiké has explained my grammar error. I do not need the first sentence to be in the "is ---ing" format. I have misread or misunderstood some ancient Common language rules. He thinks my mistakes are funny and I should "be leaving them." But from now on, these Intervals should be more correct and easier to read.

—Dzarn Reith Koras, of
Calindey's *Star Glow*

Chapter Four: Observers & Spies

I thought the Zeen showed great restraint against Corrigan, given they had murdered the Eze. Our leader had been the great love of her life.

Then I learned that despite her words about imprisonment until trial, she had begun working against the Corrigan immediately, relentlessly, at the same time she continued to build support for our fight against the Compact.

The first thing she did toward the war effort was send Zola to Jiaru to liaise with that group.

I would like to have gone there. For several reasons, not merely my desire to explore, though that was a strong part of my drive *to go*. I would like to have seen how they did things. Also, I felt it my duty.

Worse, the second thing Mother did was send me with guards to the behind-the-Falls cavern whose entrance is a state secret. Despite my strong move against the Mers rebels, Mother seemed to think I was too weak to defend myself.

I questioned why I was obeying her, even as I went. Didn't obeying make me look weak? What good, strong Eze deferred to his *mother?*

It certainly made it harder for my spies to report to me. But report they did.

The cavern is and has been for as long as our family could remember, the "safe house" for our leaders. The retreat to safety in dangerous times. I was a little surprised she hadn't sent all of us there, immediately upon the Eze's death.

Of course, Corrigan had needed to be found and dealt with. To fail to strongly respond to the assassination of our Eze would have made our leadership look shaky, prompting more rebellions. So she found the obvious traitor, then sent me away and went after the others who had betrayed our trust.

The caverns, as you might imagine, are damp and dark. The view out the cavern mouth of the sunlit falling water was the most pleasant aspect of the place. Some details of comfort had been made to the retreat over the years, for who knew how long the leadership might need to stay safe here? It was still an interim place, not home.

A ledge that ran along the south-facing cliff wall opposite the entrance to the cavern provided the sunlight needed to charge our solar lights and heat. An unobtrusive bank of solar collectors were fastened there. Periodically a trusted retainer was sent to wipe away the mist that covered the collectors, and to ensure that water-proofing gaskets and frames still did their job. So we have lights and a little heat in our cavern.

My "bedroom" is a four by three meter square space between paper screen "walls." I have a bed, a chair and a table.

I had brought six book cubes with me: one history, one written by an ecology expert about Tehassa and edited and prepared by the Oracle. Also, one picture book for teaching vocabulary and structure of the main Ayi language. The rest were fictions that I had hoped would amuse me but which I put down after a few pages.

I got up, sat down, and got up again. Seemingly too restless to figure out what I wanted to do, or where I wanted to be. And that thought stopped me cold. The *where* part. I realized I hadn't gone anywhere lately. I hadn't left the capitol city for two seasons. Montmarras is beautiful, but I had been everywhere, seen everything in the palace and the city. More than once.

And now I was trapped in an even smaller space.

I was more than ready for something new. I should have taken advantage of the uprising at our Mers home and taken the opportunity to go myself to supervise it. It would have been a change of scenery, although I've been there many times before. I sighed. Too late to regret that.

One of my guards stamped his feet outside my screen and I gave him permission to enter. He did the rest of his safety check, glancing beyond the last screen between me and the unfinished rough end of the cave. It bothered me that this "safety hideout" only has one way in or out. It would be all too easy to trap us in here, if anyone discovered our location.

At least my mother did give her permission to allow visitors.

My sister would have been permitted to come, but she was busy elsewhere.

So it was that one evening we were graced with my friend Tengda's visit for dinner. She carried a basket filled with fresh-baked bread, leaf-wrapped baked fish, and assorted squashes sauteed in a buttery sauce.

We laughed at our poor table and implements, so different from the grandeur of our formal meals in the castle. Tengda had worn a gown which must have been new, since I had not seen it before. Its gold and orange and peach stripes caught the light and made her seem to shine.

Then it was time for her to go, and one of the soldiers escorted her back up to the castle, and my small room seemed very much emptier without her.

We shielded our lights in the cavern at nighttime. As must be obvious, a glowing waterfall shining brightly in the dark of night would give away where the retreat was. So several layers of tall screens set up in a zig-zag pattern provided enough of a baffle to hide all trace of the lights deeper within. It also dimmed the natural light, so by the time I walked back to my room, it was dim and chilly.

Plass bedframes ultimately solved the problem of moldy and mildewed beds, but we'd brought dry linens with us. One of the guards and I had made up my bed. Theirs were in the next screen-sectioned "room" closer to the entrance.

The outer room, nearest the cave mouth behind the waterfall, was our sitting room and kitchen area.

We ate mostly fish stew and soups, with rough-baked multigrain bread made by one of the guards on our small solar stove.

I read books and studied the Ayi trade language. I took my spies' reports. All the while I felt like I was a mere observer of my kingdom: I might be "on the inside," but I was peering out, trying to see everything through the narrow slit of other people's reports.

I learned that, ignoring the fact we needed all the fighters we could muster for the Compact war effort, the Zeen had sent a century of cavalry across to Barque, as a move against Corrigan. Most of the two hundred I sent to Mers had returned, and some of those same people had been included in this retaliatory move against Corrigan.

Those tough men and women, fighters on horseback, surrounded Corrigans' shipyards and docks, intimidating citizens and businesspeople alike. They seized a portion of each shipment that went out or in. Most of these "tithes" as my mother called them were supplies that went for our war effort. But besides this, one of my own spies learned that my Mother negotiated with Nneka Salisu to enter a portion of those goods, or their sale price, into our own Kell coffers, for some later use.

Further, she had every Corrigan ship searched going and coming. Our soldiers found one ship, from

Yent of all places, loaded with people in chains. *Slaves.*

In the tiny meeting hall of the cavern, the three of us, the Zeen, Musa Ibrahim—Minister of the Watch (what many nations might call the Warleader or General) and I, discussed this. We tried to perceive what in all the hells Corrigan felt they must use slaves for, that they would risk kidnapping people.

Musa instructed his fighters (via courier pigeon, our fastest communication with the Inner isles) to free these kidnapped and enslaved people and return them to their homeland, once our people on Barque had questioned them. He'd already received a response.

The prospective slaves had known little about their intended service, except for a single man who said he had been commissioned at first as a trainer for hand-to-hand fighters. When he had objected to being taken to *Barque* to do so, he had been chained like the rest. So apparently, Corrigan had been in the early stages of gathering an army.

Later, I sent a note congratulating my mother for her insistence on searching the Corrigan ships.

Her response was, "You would have thought of it too, if you had a little more experience."

That gave me an unsettling look at her opinion of me as future Eze. She really did think me too immature, too inexperienced.

I began to feel offended.

After two tendays in hiding, I asked, "When do you suppose I can *safely* return to my quarters?" but she did not respond to that.

While the cavern had been updated with fresh bedding and supplies for our small kitchen, it was a far cry from comfortable. Besides, I knew I was missing events and details, despite my spies.

I even missed the silent presence of our Ayi liaison.

Eventually, one of my spies showed up with a big smile on his face. "The Zeen has sent six balloons with bombs to hit the pirate base at Vaimaey," he said. "A trial of our attack system before we fight the Compact, and a firm response to Vaimaey's constant guerrilla attacks."

"And how did it go?"

His smile was so wide, it looked like his teeth might escape. "We smashed all their headquarters buildings and supply warehouses with ease. Success!"

"Good," I said. And it *was* good to move against our plague of pirates.

But it wasn't as good a test of what we could do against the Oracle. We had no idea what kind of strength or shielding the Oracle buildings might have. Human buildings were one thing; alien-built ones were quite another.

I needed to ask our Ayi observer his opinion on this. Of course, he would never be allowed to come here, to our safe-house cave, so it would have to wait.

But my spy was still there beside me, his smile still as big as ever, reminding me of the mythical cheshire cat: white teeth shining in the darkness, a floating grin.

"Better," the guard went on, "the Zeen feels it is now safe for you to rejoin her in the palace."

She doesn't think the pirates of Vaimaey will retaliate?

Perhaps I just didn't realize the extent of the destruction at the Vaimaey pirate base, if I imagined they could mount a retaliatory strike, while she didn't.

But I did not argue with Mother or her guards. I returned to my rooms in the palace before she changed her mind.

My first action was to call the Ayi, Reith, to my office. He showed up so promptly, I almost believed he had been outside my door, awaiting my call.

"I assume you know of the balloon attack on our enemy, the pirates at Vaimaey?"

"Yes," he said simply.

"So," I said, "while it appeared successful against Human pirates, I am concerned with how we will do against the Compact forces at the Oracle with these methods."

Well, I was concerned about what help we'd be at the *Preserve* too; but there our main attack force was presumed to be the Dolphinfolk and their cousins. Sonics, *from the sound of things*, heh, were going to be much more effective than our homemade bombs.

I cleared my throat and added, "We are calling the combined fleet of ships, Dolphinfolk, whales, gymbals and Dragonfolk, along with some balloons, the *flotilla*. This is to distinguish it from our small balloon distraction attack at the Oracle."

"Yes," he said. "To be sure, your bombs will do little against the buildings or the people in them at the Oracle," Reith Koras said. The Ayi blinked, looking so Human it was easy to forget he was a member of an alien species.

He went on, "But the point is not so much to cause *damage* there, as it is to distract them, I think?"

"I wonder if that will be enough," I said, thinking aloud.

He shrugged. "When I served there, I found the other beings at the Oracle to be fairly complacent. Maybe even lazy," he added, "particularly the Simbara. Such an attack will be so unexpected, I think you will succeed with your distraction even if it is weak."

"Is there anything they can do from there to hurt the flotilla, or specifically, the Dolphinfolk and whales?"

"Even if there was, which I don't believe there is, I think they would not hurt the Dolphinfolk, who are growing into a new intelligent species that the Cuy are watching closely.

"Also, we think they will not hurt the whales, whose home this has become, and who are innocent of breaking the Compact." He chewed his lip. "I cannot promise the same against your people, but I think I am safe in saying that Simbara and Mengsee are here to observe, not control or fight. We don't *think* they will counterattack."

I nodded at him, staring, because I felt like he had something more to say.

He blinked again and rubbed his hands up and down the suede-like skin of his arms. Then he said, "There is a sonic curtain at the Oracle that will stop your bombs from damaging anything. I doubt your small bombs are strong enough to bring it down.

"But, your intent there is not to harm them, just to keep them distracted so they do not repair their satellites, so they will stay unaware of your flotilla. Thus your main group's attack on the Preserve will be hidden for as long as possible."

"Yes. Can you estimate how long we should try to keep them distracted?"

"I believe the initial surprise is all that's needed. Once my Lady's ship has usurped the Oracle's communications, it will take the...probably the Mengsee...as much as twenty minutes to become aware they aren't receiving real-time data. After they realize, it could then take them up to an hour to find and repair the blocks we will put in.

"Once the Oracle aliens see and know about the flotilla's attack on the Preserve, they possibly will call for ships to come and assist them. Possibly both modern sea-ships and sky-ships which they may have available here, will come to the Preserve to strengthen the shields around their outpost."

"All right. I'll pass that along to Zola when she returns. She should have a more exact idea of how long the rest of the Preserve attackers, particularly the Jiaru people and their ships, expect our distraction to last. We need to ensure that we all work together: our flotilla as well as our balloons at the Oracle." I thought a moment, then added, "I also need to ask the Dolphinfolk how long their attack will take to build up."

He nodded.

"Meanwhile, I'll calculate how many bombs we need to send with the Oracle group, given we only need to drop them at the beginning."

"Yes. Anything more than that will probably be wasting your time and *materiel*." It was his turn to think a minute. "Hmm...but after all, I think a second wave of bombs might be wise. It would distract them longer. We will block their communications. They will expand their barrier over the entire Oracle installation and I doubt you can do anything against that, but if their attention is on you, they will take longer to notice their communications are blocked."

I scowled, considering the barrier. All we knew about it was it was some sort of sonic screen. "Will what the Dolphinfolk and whales plan really break the barrier protecting the buildings at the Preserve, then?"

He stared at the inlaid wood of my suite's floor for a moment. Then he cleared his throat and raised his head. "My Lady is convinced they will be effective. And there are a few things she could do to add to their attack if it seems to not be enough on its own."

"I see."

"It is a sonic barrier, and their attack is sonic waves, which will disrupt the barrier."

I sighed. "Okay, if you say so."

"It is important to my people that you succeed," he revealed.

That was interesting.

"Just so what your Lady plans can prevent the Oracle group from seeing our flotilla approach the Preserve."

"That it will do."

"Thank you," I said, dismissing him.

He took the hint and left.

Mother called me to her office, "For a discussion," her note said. She did not specify a time or how much haste was needed, so I took the time to shower and dress in better clothes than I'd worn during the two tendays of my "protective imprisonment" behind the Falls.

Then I made my way to the Zeen's office.

She glanced up at me as I entered, setting down a book she had been looking at.

She then picked up a tattered letter.

"Your sister reports the Jian exiles and the so-called 'pirates' of Jiaru, including their own pack of Dragonriders, are all committed to the rebellion, just as our Dolphinfolk said."

"Good." We'd been counting on significant help from that group.

"I am going to send a pair of our Dragonriders over to take her and her guards to the Library of Humanity on their way home."

I scowled. "Can I not go? Why extend her trip when I am here doing nothing?"

"You are *not* doing *nothing*. You are *here*, being Ras L'eul for our people to see."

"They will hardly notice if I am away for a few days. I just was out of sight for two tendays, at *your* direction, hiding in a cave!"

"And that is all the more reason you need to be seen now." She glanced at my face. "Do you think you will be able to leave the country to go visiting when you are Eze?"

"It might help consolidate our power. It would certainly help me get a better feel for our people's interests and concerns."

She snorted her opinion of that idea. "Visiting other realms is what siblings are for," she said.

I tilted my head, disgust evident on my face, I am sure. "Kiké?"

"I do not send Kiké to the Library, I send your most competent sister."

"Do you think there might be something helpful there?" By changing the focus of our conversation, I could pull her attention off of me and what I might want. I hoped.

"At the very least," she said, "I want an *exact* copy of any documents that may exist there about the Compact itself, as well as the specific Rules of Settlement for Azureign. We believe the aliens have broken the Compact, but it would be good to have real documentation of their promises from the beginning times, to contrast with the reality, now."

I nodded. "What about our Ayi friend? Has he had any suggestions?"

"That *was* his suggestion, in part. He also told me that each First-In family has a treasure there."

I knew from all my reading—and Kiké's—that our family, K!elli! or Kell, had been among those first settlers on Azureign.

Corrigan, interestingly, had not been. Not just our enemies were missing from that list, though: La!lima had not been First-In, nor others of our friends. TenStar was, and Lawal and Salisu. Did she intend to steal their family treasures?

"Do we need money so badly?" I hated showing ignorance, but I honestly had thought my family was quite wealthy.

"We are fine, but our nation is not. War is expensive, as Salisu keeps reminding us. The Ayi representative also recommended ways to limit access to the Library so our enemies cannot access what is there. Well, and to protect against our ally Jiaru's enemies grabbing everything there, too."

I said nothing, diving down the rabbit hole in my mind of consequences and beliefs that the Library information was *for all Humanity upon Azureign.*

If we limit it, aren't we abusing our power? What will happen when others find out we'd prevented them from accessing their birthright?

On the other hand, letting the information our ancestors had hidden there for us to find fall into the hands of our enemies—real and vicious pirates, along with Corrigan—well, that would be foolish too.

Perhaps she was correct, but it seemed risky to me.

She shook her head. "Our old thorn-in-hoof problem, your cousin Zohany, is well-established in Farnesse, you might recall. She was divested from Kell and exiled from Tehassa for exactly her covetous desire to claim the Library for herself when it was discovered.

"I have sent guards to the Library on permanent assignment. Other nations will or have already sent some of theirs also, to hold the Library in neutrality. Our soldiers have been sent in your name, as this is something you should have taken care of."

"I see." She had already done this, without even bothering to inform me, while I was parked safely behind the waterfall—out of her way.

I suppose it was good she wanted to keep the Library and all it held safe from my ex-cousin Zohany and her pirate affiliates.

But she kept making decisions with even bothering to consult with me, and announced them to me after the fact, as if it should have been me doing it. It has to be obvious to our various advisors and representatives from our other Isles that the Zeen is running things, not me.

I don't mind not being in charge as much as I mind being *blamed* for not being in charge. Did she expect me to lock her away in a cell and take over as Eze?

There was a slow burn that wanted to start, a resentment against her manipulations. She seized power at my father's death, and showed no sign of relinquishing it, even as she chided me for not being strong or smart or active or experienced enough to be Eze, changing the descriptor of my failings as it suited her.

Was this because I quietly followed her order to sequester myself in our secret safe-house? I am fairly certain if I had refused to go, even so far as struggling against the guards, she would then have chided me for being childish.

Either way, she got what she wanted. An excuse to continue in charge, me removed from decisions.

Finally I shrugged and walked away. My sister was already on her way to visit the Library of Humanity, never mind how useful it would have been for me to go.

And now I knew the Library was being protected by soldiers from all over Azureign, and that is a good thing, if it works.

Besides, I suppose it is possible there would be nothing helpful there, at least for this coming war. Was it going to have a list of helpful suggestions for staging a rebellion against our interdiction? How useful could millennium-old information be against starships?

Beyond these truths, we already know we have a secret weapon, that not even Jiaru's Red or our Corrigan and pirate enemies know about: The Dolphinfolk and their cousins' *sonics.*

This ability, as far as I can tell from all my historical and biological readings, is *new*. It developed on Azureign, from some basic sonic communication abilities the whales and dolphins had had on Earth. The Humans who built the Library wouldn't have known about that.

Nor would they have known we have allies in the Compact.

I didn't even consider what the Ayi might bring to the fight. Reith has been quiet but assured about their ability to assist us. They seem tremendously powerful, to me. Even if Zola found that the Library of Humanity had nothing useful to add, I began to think our revolt could succeed.

My spies discovered the Zeen had seized ten of Corrigan's ships and had them sailed to our harbor.

I could in no way comprehend how those were useful to our war effort. Yes, we were sailing every Ocean-side ship we owned to the Preserve. But these ships were Sea-side: that is, above the falls, not below them. Did she have some plan to get them down the falls? Or were they intended as home support?

She called me to her office.

"I assume you have calculated how many cannons, sails, and so forth we will need?"

"I still don't have a solid estimate of the number of ships we'll have available to send," I said.

"I am determined to provide fifty."

"So a total of 100 cannons, plus the sails and ropes, water barrels and desalinators, food and clothing for sailors on those fifty."

She nodded.

"We're close with sails and other supplies. We're still short on cannons."

She nodded again. "Strip the Corrigan ships of those and send them down. Does that get us closer?"

"Musa managed to capture six from the pirate ships at Vaimaey," I said, adding them up in my head. "If the Corrigans have at least ten, we should be good. More would be better, though."

"Have you ordered enough balls and gunpowder to fire them?"

"Yes, of course. The last shipment is due to arrive tomorrow from Sawad Shati in Old Maladh, and it is our last ship scheduled to join us also. I think that gives us only 49."

"I'll order the biggest Corrigan ship lifted down, then."

I was startled by this. "Do you really think an Inner Sea boat is going to survive on the Azure Ocean?"

She was nodding even before I finished speaking. "This one is their 'flagship' you might say. Reinforced beams, a deeper hull—I think it was meant for ocean use, but they never got it lifted down to the ocean harbor. In any event, it is our fiftieth ship. How are you distributing the balloons? Are we tethering them to the bigger ships and keeping them aloft?"

Again I was startled. I shook my head, staring at her face; its bland expression told me nothing about what she was thinking.

"It is not a good idea to tow inflated balloons. It may make our ships impossible to push across the ocean. And more, there is no reason for it. The balloons will be shipped in pieces and assembled as we approach the Preserve."

She nodded, a small smug smile on her lips.

I wasn't sure what she felt smug about; *she* hadn't realized we shouldn't tow inflated balloons.

I went on, "I have spread them out across two dozen of our ships, those long enough to properly lay out the envelopes. The gear for inflating them has likewise been distributed to those ships, most of which are set up for two balloons each."

"Only forty-eight?"

"All we have envelopes for, since the hangar fire."

Her lips pouched into a grimace. But whatever she thought, she didn't voice it.

"How soon do we depart?" I asked, since no one had bothered to tell me.

"Zola said the Jiaru group is planning to leave within a tenday," she said.

"By then we may have three or four more balloons, though I don't have ships long enough to accommodate them." The silk has to be straight, without tangles or folds.

"Put them all aboard the Corrigan freighter, then; it's big enough."

I sighed. "All right," I said. "Who is crewing it?"

"Jiaru sailors will be mixed with our own experienced people; we still have more sailors than ships."

"Good," I said.

She nodded, then waved me off.

Besides these practical preparations, and without knowing how effective it would ever be, I continued practicing my "distancing" effect that Mother's guidance counselor had suggested I try, to control my focus issues.

That is, I try to take a step back (figuratively) and look at a bigger picture. If I was ever going to be as perceptive as Mother and Zola were, I needed to learn how to increase the span of my focus. I needed to "zoom out" as we did with our telescopes, to see a larger, though less-detailed view, and then teach myself how to assemble that additional information into a meaningful whole.

While I was assembling balloons and ships and working on expanding my view, I was also watching the Zeen's actions and awaiting the return of my sister. Even with all that, we had a threat that none of us saw coming.

Chapter Five: Attack on our Sovereignty

I was so relieved to be out of the caverns behind the Falls that I spent a few hours one day riding the gondolas across to Isubu Omi and back, just to see something besides waterfall and the insides of caverns and my quarters in Montmarras. I would like to have gone all the way to Mers, but discovered the gondola cables were under repair.

The cable engineers were not certain if it was "normal wear and tear" or if there had been sabotage, but at least they'd caught it before there had been an accident.

Gondolas have the advantage of not relying on the wind, but instead use the power generated by the falls themselves. They can't carry much besides a few people, and are hazardous in bad weather, but are a useful backup to balloons and boats. The currents around the falls are treacherous. It didn't even occur to me to try sailing across the narrow strait.

This little journey gave me time to organize my thoughts and to write up a checklist of everything that must be done to supply ourselves for our part in the rebellion, as well as a shorter but still important list to ensure the well-being and safety of our people who remained behind.

I added the names of the persons responsible for each item or action. Later I would ensure they'd followed through. I was fairly comfortable that all had been done, but sometimes the stupidest little detail could derail a plan, and we had many plans which must interlock properly with the other people and the Dolphinfolks' plans.

Besides ensuring our population was cared for, I hoped to find enough money to set up pensions to go to any families who lost members in this action, or who had to deal with disabling injuries. Freedom has a cost too often overlooked.

To get more money into Tehassa's coffers, I needed to find new products for us to sell, that wouldn't violate the terms of the Fair and Balanced Economy regulations.

After thinking about that for awhile, I realized two things: first, if the rebellion failed, I had no idea what the consequences would be—such as whether our nation of Tehassa would even *exist* afterwards. It wouldn't matter what the state of our treasury was.

The second was that if our rebellion succeeded, we *no longer would be constrained by any of the Compact rules!* This astonishing idea left me with so many potentialities I had to set them aside. I could perhaps think about this more during our sail to the Preserve.

We would be able to export anything and everything we could produce. What a novel idea!

The only move I actually made when I returned from my gondola ride, was to set two of my office assistants to researching and creating charts of the global economy as it now stands. They were to show which nations were richest and why. Some of them were earning from resources we simply did not have— so far as we knew—but there were others we could take advantage of and/or duplicate.

We could also prospect our Isles and mainland holdings to see what hidden resources they might hold.

I still remembered reading about the amethyst geode a couple lucky fishermen had found in the caves below the falls at Mers. They'd gone into the cave for protection from a storm, and had come out with a double fist-sized rock worth thousands of credits to a collector in Maladh. Perhaps there were more. And that was just one tiny example of discoveries we might make once free of the alien restrictions.

I put one of those two young assistants in charge of researching refrigeration systems, too, and what was required to build, use and maintain them. One simple way we could earn more was to be able to export our seafood throughout Azureign. First we must construct better ways to preserve it for shipping, and combine that with faster shipping methods. We'd require faster, stronger ships anyway, without the Dolphinfolk to help push them through Azureign's stupidly strong oceans. Maybe the Ayi knew of fuels that would produce engines that would be faster or more powerful than our little solar-powered ones while still being ecologically sound.

We had some seafood items in Tehassa that were rare even along the vast western coast of our supercontinent, in what had been Jia and Maladh. Even the Archipelago did not have red snapper, which could often sell for exorbitant rates in Lynly. That was just one fish, to one nation.

If our rebellion failed? Well, that was far more difficult to predict, so I did not waste much time on it. It was unknowable, but would probably no longer be my problem, if I even survived. At the back of my mind, also, was the Compact's threat to remove us all from Azureign if we warred. Then our circumstances would most assuredly be different. If they could even do such a thing.

Having checked our preparations and set some new research into motion, I gave myself permission to secure a spot in one of the balloons that circuit our islands. I wanted to be absent from Montmarras for several days.

I did not want to go so far as Vaimaey, which is still a big trouble spot for our nation, but I would be happy to look over our eight major isles to see what was new and how our people and crops were doing. The circular wind gyre around our Isles established our balloon trade route. Outer Isles prevailing winds go west. Inner Isles winds go east. So we have balloons that run the circle, or elongated oval, really.

This did not satisfy my desire to see something new, but at least it was travel. At least it was going somewhere, without the niceties of court to attend to.

I completely enjoyed myself on that longer journey, even as I used that time to make other lists, lists of things that were of interest *to me*, or needed doing, or that I should talk to the Zeen or the Ayi about, for our peoples' sakes.

I think we were all feeling fairly complacent, since there had been no reprisals for the Zeen's attack on Vaimaey, and my sister had safely arrived at the Library. Our guards had peacefully been integrated with the other national guards to protect the Library.

I returned from my balloon circuit refreshed and with new ideas.

Things were going well, so we were off our guard.

Every other tenday, my brother goes among our people to distribute food, dry goods, and sometimes a little money to the people. He would roll his chair out to the southern courtyard of the palace, and guards would monitor the gates, letting in one or two people at a time.

It was perhaps a cruel job to give to the guards, but they were to look over the supplicants and let in whomever seemed to need our charity the most. And also to ensure that it wasn't the same people, repeating their visit each twenty-day. We wanted everyone to have a chance.

Kiké listened to the people's needs and distributed what we hoped was a helpful dispensation in each case. Usually it is a particular kind of food. That is, our people are not necessarily starving, but they had come to Tehassa so long ago with the preferences of their own, original, tribes *on Earth,* and we do not grow much of an assortment of grains here in Tehassa.

Our land is wet and cloudy much of the time, which is not a good environment for wheat and corn, for example, which prefer a sunnier and drier growing season than we have. We import most of our grains. We grow rice on the sunnier Inner Isles; enough for our own people but not to export.

We do export certain tropical fruits, flowers, and the most transportable of the vegetable crops we can grow. Many of these are shipped while unripe, as it can take two tendays to barge it across the Inner Sea. Also we have a small portion of our arable land committed to hardwoods for both our own use, and for export. All these things helped add to our treasury, so that we have funds for charity and to do what is needed for our people.

So the people who came to Kiké asking for corn got five kilos of dried corn kernels in a bag. Similarly for wheat, both of which we import from the vast fields on the Kendai plains, and some also from Yent or Lhasa, depending on what the weather has done to their crops and who has an unexpected bounty.

Others of our people ask Kiké for cloth, usually to make clothes with, but sometimes for linens or other use. As far as I know, there are no mills anywhere on Azureign for making cloth on a large scale. Many households have their own hand looms and spend evenings spinning thread or weaving cloth. While we have a few steam-driven looms for weaving fine silk, it is still expensive and slow to produce. While silk is not included in our alms, its sale to outsiders does pay for the other things we give our neediest people.

So this is a thing that Kiké looks forward to doing, and it frees the rest of us to do other work.

That day, I was sourcing shotgun pellets, things with which I was wholly unfamiliar. We had a few guns around the palace, "just in case" weapons. These were used so seldom I couldn't even find records of where we'd gotten the pellets to load them with.

At the Preserve, we did not expect shotguns to be as useful as our cannons, for we were knocking down buildings, not shooting people. But it was felt at least a few should be brought to protect our seamen, and that might also be useful for hunting sea birds while we sailed. Even sailors can get tired of fish.

I was examining a pamphlet about quality signatures on these pellets, and where they could be bought, when I heard an uproar outside.

While my rooms overlook the inner courtyard of our palace, my office gets the poorer view to the south, which includes the southern courtyard...where Kiké was.

A quick glimpse out the window showed there was a mob *inside the gates* and surrounding Kiké, having apparently overwhelmed the guards. I couldn't even *see* my little brother through the rowdy mob.

I did see a few people, dressed as peasants, who raised whips. I say "dressed as peasants" because even I could see from so far away that how they moved meant they were trained fighters, not ordinary people. No, they were soldiers or pirates in peasant dress that swung their fists or spun and kicked in a soldierly way. A few used a weird kind of whip to clear their path. These weren't any peasants of ours.

As I ran down the stairs to the ground floor, I could hear the boots of various guards heading that way also. I hoped some of them, at least, got there before I did, because I had no idea how to fight against so many people. Those whips made me worry about how many of them might be armed in other ways as well. But I would get my brother out of there if I could.

As I got closer, I could see the "peasants" indeed had whips that they were using, striking wildly among the crowd. I could see also that those whips left a sparkling light-effect trail behind as their wielders swung and struck. I had never seen such things before.

Did they have blades attached to them that caught the sunlight? All I knew was whoever they hit with those whips did not rise again.

I saw a couple of our larger guards plowing a path through the people as I ran toward them. I still could not see Kiké. The people were chanting unintelligible phrases; I finally realized there were two opposing groups, one chanting "No war no!!" and others countering with, "Freedom from the Bugs!"

Who had decided the Compact aliens were bugs, I never found out, but it made a great image, I suppose. Especially since some of them *are* rather insectoidal, not that our people had ever seen them. Not even we of family Kell had seen them, though some individual people who have visited the Oracle have gotten a glimpse.

I saw one of our guards, a large, muscular man with shining ebony skin, just *tossing* people aside as he made his way to my brother. I got a glance at Kiké, who was bent down in his chair, his arms covering his head. His arms had bloody streaks on them. He was terrified.

And he was at risk of further harm, from our own people!

The huge guard grabbed the handles of the wheelchair and began rolling my brother toward the palace, the people still swarming around us and chanting. One of the whip-carriers was making his way toward the guard with my brother. I approached, trying to cut the whip-wielder off from Kiké.

No one else seemed to be fighting, for a wonder, though they did continue to chant and get in the way.

I slid in and took over pushing the chair so the guard could clear a way through. Two others of our guards grabbed the man wielding the sparkling whip; one was hit by it and fell, the other grabbed the man's arm and wrenched the whip free, throwing it far away.

There were tears streaking Kiké's face when we finally got him safely inside.

The Zeen was there just inside the doorway, where she bent over Kiké's chair to assure herself of her youngest son's safety. He had some scratches on his arms and face, and a big bruise was rising on his forehead where someone's bony fist or elbow had clipped him.

One of the household aides ran up and took over Kiké's chair, murmuring, "Infirmary." She rolled him away. He turned and gave me one sad look as he disappeared down the hall. He was hurt and confused. I stayed behind to speak to my mother.

Ignoring me, the Zeen signaled the guards, and stepped outside the door. She raised the shotgun she had carried that I hadn't even noticed. She shot into the air, one crashing loud boom of both barrels, which was followed by an abrupt silence, even as the shot echoed across the stony courtyard.

"Shame on you!" she called, in her reverberating "address the people" voice. "Go *home!* If you must protest, do it in the city square. I will hear you. Or, write a letter to the crown! Seek an audience! But do not threaten my family like this!"

She looked across the crowd and back.

"Never have I been so ashamed of Tehassa!" She turned away and came back inside the palace, out of their sight. Probably only I and maybe a guard saw the line of sweat run down her dark face and neck before she used her sleeve to wipe it away.

I watched the crowd as the guards tried to press the door closed. Most of the people were cringing away, embarrassed.

A few turned and made rude gestures, among them two other whip carriers, and I grabbed the head guard's telescope, to find and examine those faces, committing them to memory. Then the door was closed and I could see nothing of who was there. I handed the guard back his telescope.

Of course we permit dissent. This is not a tyranny.

But to attack my brother, on Alms Day?

I had a feeling there was more to this than a few disgruntled anti-war citizens, or even this atypical mob of them, seeded with fake peasants.

Group insanity we were familiar with, though it did not happen often.

Someone was instigating this aggression. It did not feel like "just" a few anti-war protestors. Could it be foreign influence? I began to think so, if for no other reason than those *whips*. I'd never seen such a thing before, like harnessed lightning. Where had they gotten such a thing? Who was doing this?

Could it be Corrigan, striking back at my family? The perfidious Zohany? It took awhile, but we did eventually find out.

It turned out to be much worse than Corrigan.

Chapter Six: Our True Fight Begins

Zola returned from the Library of Humanity, where she had gone after visiting Jiaru and the Pirate Queen.

She had news that turned our rather naive notions about the Compact aliens upside down.

We had long believed the alien peoples who made up the Compact were basically benign. We had thought the Compact peoples meant well toward Humanity and us here on Azureign.

We are now learning otherwise.

They have their own agendas and are enacting them. Now that we are aware, we are discovering in how many ways they have affected us.

We now must learn how to enable our own priorities and overcome theirs.

Zola found a Timeline that showed explorers from Earth had discovered Azureign millennia *before* the Compact aliens ever made contact with Humanity.

They had no right to tell us what we could do with this planet, which had been considered part of Earth's holdings since the beginning of our species' journeys out into the galaxy away from our home system.

The Compact members had simply been indignant because we had dared to terraform a world that might have been the nest for another intelligent species to rise from. Eventually. In a few billion years. Maybe.

Or, perhaps they had hoped to make it a colony of their own.

Perhaps.

So, they had been angry about what *might have been,* arguing that we had possibly destroyed a species that might have come to exist—or not.

And then they behaved as if they had the absolute right to punish us for it.

Our own people played a part in this, too.

Why had Earth ever signed the Compact agreement? And more especially, why had they agreed to sacrifice *our* planet in exchange for the dubious advantages of membership in the alien group?

This never became clear to me.

At that time, the time of the signing, Humanity had established ten other colonies on habitable planets they had found. Perhaps they felt they needn't support the eleventh. Perhaps there had been an enemy unknown to us, that the Compact protected them from, I don't know.

Perhaps if we had been permitted to communicate with our fellow Humans on Earth, or even other colonies, we might know this.

Then there was another bit of the Library information that puzzled me almost as much: Only two additional Human colonies had been founded *after* the Compact was signed. That was an enormous slow-down from the original pace of colonization from Earth.

Of course we had no idea if there had been other colonies established since our interdiction, for we had been out of contact with Earth for a very long time now, but it was a disturbing trend. Eleven colonies in the two thousand years before the Compact (and after Human space exploration began, of course), but only two more in the thousand years since—that we had records of.

I had no way to know, perhaps there had been many more since then. It still represented a significant deceleration in the spread of Humanity. Was the Compact limiting them as well as us? Had our home planet's explorers come up against other species' claims? Was none of the Compact signatories willing to share planets and star systems? Must they leave them all untouched? I had no way to know, unless the Ayi were willing to explain. I made a note to ask Reith.

Of course, the biggest question to me was, why had Earth given Azureign up? This might be something Reith or his Lady would not know.

Yes, Azureign is my home, and I naturally think it is beautiful. It is also unique, in that it has rings that as far as we now know, no other colony world has.

But after all, these puzzlements are diversions I must set aside for now. They are no help to our war effort, just further questions I wished we had answers for about our place—indeed, Humanity's place—in the galaxy.

While Zola was unable to make copies of the locked up—but visible—original Compact contracts and edicts, she did read them and take careful notes. We all examined those closely.

Our best claim that the aliens had broken the Compact was information that our Human life span was distinctly shorter than it had been *even at the time of settlement.*

Shorter!

This was the result of the interdiction and its limitations. We'd been prevented from developing any medical advances beyond the most primitive of the practices the rest of Humanity had left behind centuries ago.

We were also not allowed to *research* our resources to determine if we colonists were getting a proper balance of nutrients and trace minerals in our Azureign diet.

Both these factors had undoubtedly contributed to our shortened life spans.

Besides this, both Zola and the Jiaru boy who had visited the Library independently, also found out we had virtually no protection against disease. Neither did our food crops, though we had been meticulous with our organic methods to control and contain disease and predators on our plantings throughout the centuries. Knowing you are interdicted tends to make you careful about such things.

To make the argument short: many Azureign colonists had died of weaknesses from imbalanced nutrition and long-known diseases *that had not needed to.*

This so shocked my Mother that she retreated to her quarters for an entire morning. Thinking about Kiké, I would imagine.

While these limits on our health and population apparently are acceptable to our alien oversight committee, they *enraged* us and our people.

Of course we who were suffering from their high and mighty rules were angry. What else would they expect? They'd deliberately kept us in ignorance about the matter, too. I guess they supposed they had enough control over us that they never expected us to find out how much we had been limited.

It was clear to me that the Library of Humanity and its holdings had not been taken into account when the Compact was signed on Azureign. They— that is, the Compact aliens—had all thought we would remain innocent of any of this information...because I honestly believe, they *knew at heart* if we discovered it, we would rebel.

Further, the aliens promised in their Compact agreements called Duties of the Oracle, to *"protect and ensure the well-being of all populations on any interdicted world."*

So this is an obvious conflict: Preventing us from discovering inoculations and more advanced healing methods was most clearly *NOT* protecting and ensuring our well-being!

Zola also discovered that the Priestesses, Azureign's answer to the directive that we "...must establish and maintain at least one Oversight organization, as religious or political or military, to enforce the <u>Compact and Rules of Settlement</u>, enforce <u>Ecological Balances,</u> and adjust <u>Fair and Balanced Economies."</u>

Our Priestesses do in fact oversee Azureign, and, at least in the past, have reported to the Oracle. This means we have had *two* oversight organizations ensuring *we* didn't do anything wrong.

There was nothing in the rules to ensure our supervisors and the alien Compact members didn't do injury to us. Nothing was said about limits on how the Compact rules negatively affected colonists, or how "reasonable care" was to be defined.

Thankfully, because of the information from the Library and their own observations, the Priestesses now have recognized in the many ways the Compact is not in Humanity's favor.

The Priestesses have changed leadership.

They have joined the rebellion against the Compact and refuse to communicate with the Oracle aliens.

The last helpful information from Jiaru was that Zola had knowledge of the sparking whips we'd seen on Alms Day. Tae, the Queen of the Jiaru pirates, had told my sister that those same whips had been used against the Dolphinfolk as long ago as the coup in Lyang City. The whips had been carried there by the fighters in Red, who had also used them later to attack the remnants of her family. Here they'd been used against our people by fake, implanted peasants.

This made an undeniable link between the Red who attacked Jia and hounded the Tingh, and the imposters who had attacked my brother.

They were *new technology*, which suggested those weapons had come from the Oracle, or by some other means had been brought here from off-planet. They were nothing we'd had or ever seen on Azureign before, everyone agreed about that.

This pointed a particularly large finger at the Compact aliens. They must be the ones behind *both* the Red usurpation in Jia and the attacks on us at Tehassa.

Reith Koras had been present during these discussions, and at the end I glanced at him, wondering if he had known about the Compact's involvement, wondering if he and his Lady were part of this.

I was determined to confront him at my first opportunity.

When Zola finished reporting what she had learned at Jiaru and at the Library, she had one thing to say to me directly. A more personal thing, which she saved to tell me as she followed me to my rooms.

She said, "It would make good sense to consider marriage with Tingh Tae Lha, the Queen of Jiaru."

Now my blasted sister was trying to marry me off, too. "Oh. Yes," I responded. "Marry a pirate, our most profound of enemies." She ignored my sarcastic tone.

"The people of Jiaru aren't pirates in any real sense of the word. They are completely unconnected with the pirates at Vaimaey. The Jiaru people have done some raids against their enemies. They have beaten off attacks by the Red, and have helped fight off what we might call highwaymen. The pirates of Vaimaey—*our* evil pirates—are a completely different beast, much more like the Red who usurped the leadership in Jia and Maladh."

As if I was a naughty child, Zola shook her finger at me. "The Queen of Jiaru is our strongest ally against both our own pirates and against the forces of the Compact. We *will* help them. *They* will help us. Not to mention you and she both have a need to marry. Simple," here she brushed her hands off, "and done."

I made a face at her. "If you are in such a rush to marry one of us off, why don't *you* marry her?"

"I love someone else. You don't."

There wasn't much I could say to that. While I was fond of a couple of ladies I'd known for years, it was the fondness of siblings or friends, not love. Certainly not women I would care to romance, or could imagine living my life with.

Zola, on the other hand, had loved Dezmon since she had met him at a Montmarras Isle fair when they were both twelve. I give him no surname, because he hasn't one. Zola was still negotiating with Mother for permission to wed him. I think she may care more for Dezmon than she does her own family, and positively more than for any of the wealthy young men who have courted her—in vain.

We will see. I will meet Tingh Tae Lha, called Queen of Pirates, when we combine our fleets to begin the crossing to the Preserve.

We did not know if the Preserve had existed previously on the "original" Azureign, or if it was newly uplifted as a result of plate movement or volcanic action due to the *terraforming* that was done. All we knew for certain was that it was on the opposite side of the planet from the supercontinent, and that it was supposed to have been left pristine to develop whatever endemic plants and animals it naturally could.

Meanwhile we had more important things to consider. Like aliens provoking a war.

Before she left my suite, Zola handed me a small linen sack filled with book cubes. "Peace offering," she said. "Books from Earth."

The next morning, I took the opportunity to go down the cliff via gondola to our shore beside the Azure Ocean. None of us had recently spoken with Stormflyer pod, which are the Dolphinfolk in charge of assembling the war effort.

On my way down, I was passed by one of the big freight gondolas going back up. Its work was plain: there were a half-dozen more ships in our harbor adjacent to the base of the Falls. Soon all of the most useful parts of the captured Corrigan ships would end up down here, to be fitted onto ocean-going ships.

We had now also recalled any of our ships that had been stranded in distant ports by the Dolphinfolk revolt, so they could likewise be prepared for war. The Dolphinfolk were willing to help get these ships home to us, since they were meant for the war effort. The war that the Dolphinfolk themselves had incited, and we Dirt People had joined.

I reached the water and called for Singaree— Stormflyer's contact with us. The response was from a strange-to-me female, who was tail-standing out in the deep water. She informed me that we had been assigned Whreng! pod as our liaison, now. Stormflyer's personnel was all too involved in organizing Dolphinfolk and Dirt People and whale participants.

So this was Ingda, who rose from the waves at the deepest edge of the beach and greeted me. Ingda shared her abbreviated genealogy with me, and I gave her the short version of mine.

"We need more ships!" she abruptly switched topics and surprised me with her declaration.

"There's a few more to come," I told her. "Your pods are bringing back three more of our trade ships that we found stuck in various ports. Those will be fitted with cannons and supplies."

She seemed mollified by this, but then asked, "How many boom-shoots?" This is their word for cannons. I don't know why they both have and use their own words for some things, while for others they adopt—or adapt—our Dirt People words. Maybe cannon is too hard to say?

I keep meaning to study the Folk vocal tract and its physical characteristics, but never seem to remember, at least not when I have the time to do so.

"We promised Whiyira there would be two cannons per ship," I said. Ingda should know this, so I had to wonder what else was behind her question.

"How many ships?"

Well, she wanted the total. Which I did not know. "We are not certain how many ships will make it here in time to be fitted with cannons before we begin our sail, but we have at least fifty already prepared, so one hundred boom-shoots."

"Flotilla leaves in half of one of your tendays," she said, to meet the others from Jiaru and other places."

"Yes. We still need to establish a way to coordinate with the Oracle group and the Ayi."

"You have many, many balloons?"

I didn't bother to try and explain our setback with the hangar fire and the destruction of nearly a hundred envelopes. "We will have..." I did a quick calculation, "about one ten of pods of balloons." Meaning (I hoped) we would have a total of about sixty balloons going to the Preserve. Or close to it.

"Plus, also we will use three pods of balloons at the Oracle, most of which are already on their way there."

Ingda shrugged, which I wasn't sure whether she was applying to my last statement, or the whole conversation.

"Does that answer your questions?" I asked.

She shrugged again, flapping her flippers in the air.

"It is well," she squeaked. "Meet again in two darks," she said. "Then once again, when we leave."

"The day after tomorrow," I agreed. "And again in five darks."

She did a tail-stand and twist that meant "Agree and goodbye," and then swam rapidly away.

That evening, back at the palace, at least one of my remaining questions was answered, as Reith, the Ayi liaison, called us to meet. The Lady Calindey's little skyship showed up out of nowhere. It simply popped into existence in our hidden garden courtyard at the center of the palace.

The ship landed on the grassy area surrounded by Mother's beautiful peony and fern garden. I hoped Calidey's pilot had been careful not to crush anything. *Mother*—not the Zeen—had spent a year planning, planting and caring for that garden. The results were spectacular in the spring when the peonies bloomed, and were a lovely green retreat the rest of the time.

Lady Calindey stepped out onto the little ramp that gives her a way to get to the ground from the doorway, which is about a third of the way up the curved wall of her—supposedly small—ovoid shuttle ship. It seemed large to me, so I had to wonder how big her main ship *Star Glow* was.

Our liaison attended her, seeming to materialize next to her out of wherever he'd been previously, to greet her. He escorted her to the center of the courtyard and the table where we often had our war-planning meetings outdoors.

I knew he had been spending a lot of time with my little brother Kiké, *liaising*, I suppose. He clearly had known Calindey was coming ahead of time.

I had not. However my mother had been notified at the same time I had, and we had arrived at the courtyard table together, just in time to see the Ayi shuttle settle.

Calindey approached. She and the Zeen bowed to one another.

"I sorrow for your loss," the Ayi lady said to Mother, acknowledging my father's death.

"Thank you," Mother said with a small head-only bow. "We have discovered the assassins and removed them. Also we are in the process of rooting out the troublemakers that incited the mob against my younger son."

"He is well?"

I could see Mother's visible flinch. Kiké was in no way "well," but of course, the Ayi was asking about the effects of the near-riot on Alms Day, not his general health.

"Well enough," Mother said, "as your Reith Koras must have told you." Then Mother transformed from a mother back into the Zeen, stiffening her posture and looking Lady Calindey in the eye. "We suspect Compact agitators have incited much if not all of the unrest in our nation," she announced. I nodded my firm agreement.

This, I think, shocked the Ayi woman. She stood still, head tilted, eyes distant. Then she straightened and looked back at the Zeen. "While this is possible, I cannot offer any explanation for why they would do such a thing. It has always been our understanding— and our own observation—that they monitor, only. They do not interact, except at the Oracle."

Maybe the Red had asked the Oracle for weapons? And been given the whips? It certainly hadn't occurred to any of our own people to ask for weapons when visiting the Oracle. They were kind of banned, weren't they?

Zola spoke up. "We were told by the people at Jiaru that we should watch out for foreign spies." Zola bit her lip, then went on. "While we personally have not been to the Oracle to physically see any of the species there, we have heard descriptions by Rangers and Dragonriders who *have* been there." Calindey nodded at this, and Zola went on, "We are fairly certain we have found what must be a Toridani spy, since they were nothing like the descriptions of Simbara or Mengsee that we have been told about."

"I have never seen a Toridani person," Reith said.

Lady Calindey nodded at him, then at us. "As a species, their individuals are extremely reluctant to reveal themselves. They are much more apt to appear as a group, and that only rarely. What did you see?"

Zola shook her head. "I did not see it, Kiké did, at the edge of the crowd in the courtyard."

I took over. "This creature was pretending to be a horse, and it was a good illusion, but somehow, our little brother Kiké saw through...a *thin* spot, as he described it. That is, a see-through place in the illusion, or "horse costume," that the being had put on.

"Kiké saw a blurry sort of...octopus."

The Ayi Lady exchanged glances with Reith, then turned to us with a smile. "Thank you. That is extremely helpful information," she said. "Please thank your brother. It *was* very likely a Toridani, one of their Adventurer class. They have many classes or races, each of which looks different. They have equipment that can project a holographic field to disguise their appearance, which can frighten other species, especially interdicted ones. The Toridani are sensitive to this. I am surprised and sorry you were exposed to such a visit. I cannot explain it."

Her gaze lost focus, then she went on, "The octopoid Adventurers are the Toridani species most of us have seen, along with the warriors, who are insectoid, a few of whom work at the Oracle."

She glanced away from us, then back. "Additionally, in trade negotiations and Compact meetings *I* have met their diplomats, who are much more fish-like, and must interface with us through their water tanks—in which they must stay immersed."

Then she put her slim hand against her chest and blinked several times, eyes distant again. "But why they would try to incite rebellion among your people...?"

Reith suggested, "Perhaps they understand you are considering war against the Compact, and believe they can distract you from that."

Calindey glared at him, shutting him up. Then she looked back at us. "He should not be saying such things, but he is not wrong. Possibly by creating rebellion among your citizens, the Toridani and other Compact members hoped to dissuade you from revolt."

She shook her head "no" in the Human gesture. "But that they are trying to cause war within your nation—and meanwhile also appear to be supporting the Red against Jia—is something we find so incomprehensible, we have difficulty believing it is truly happening.

"There have been so many independent reports of this, that we must begin to believe." She then glanced at me and my sister, and then back at the Zeen.

"We may all have misinterpreted Toridani behavior in this, but I will see what I can discover. Certainly Mengsee and Simbara have different goals than we or

Toridani do. I suppose that could explain such behavior." She bowed and turned to walk back to her ship.

"Meanwhile," she called, pausing in her departure, and turning back to us, "if there is anything we need to know before you sail to the Preserve, please tell Reith and he will let me know." She bowed again and walked back to her ship, leaving us to think about many things.

Her last comment, tossed out as she left, rather confirmed that she and Reith have some way to quickly communicate with one another, as we suspected. That was good, since Reith could quickly relay our last-minute needs.

I kicked myself for not bringing up the communication problems we had. Could Reith relay instructions and timing between the Preserve and the Oracle and her ship?

Meanwhile, we would work furiously to get as many armed ships into the water as possible before assembly day, where our flotilla would gather with the others before we all head across the Ocean to the Preserve.

We also hoped to get another few balloon envelopes sewn and sealed, as backup both at the Oracle, and some to add to our boats to function as more eyes in the sky and to help us communicate between ships. The flotilla might be so spread out we would be unable to see our standard flag-message system, and the balloons could act as relays.

Then we just needed to count down the days until we reached what the Dolphinfolk had set as our Departure Day.

And eventually, Attack Day. That would happen once we had gotten ourselves across half the world's ocean, and the Oracle group had their balloons set up.

Then, we would begin our war.

INTERVAL: The Ayi Weakness

Pejiin: the Ayi blessing and curse.

This sense has guided us for so long, not using it would be like asking another species to cut off one or more of its limbs or, perhaps, two of its senses. But we do not have that choice: it exists, like breathing.

We use it to know how each other are feeling. We use it to guide us in gauging the feelings of other species, particularly those whose languages we do not know well.

Pejiin screens, which (rather like headphones can help control sound volume) do not entirely remove the effects of emotional reactions from this sense. The screens do dull the effects enough that "normal" Ayi can withstand a fight and its effects of injury and death that resonate within *pejiin* at least for awhile.

With lengthy and serious training, a few of our people can overcome and ignore *pejiin* responses, and so can work as tactical personnel—also known as gunners or starfighters. For a short period of time, they may be able to do this.

Afterwards, they are incapable of receiving normal *pejiin* responses for the remainder of their lives, and are often driven insane. Certainly, they are *considered* insane at worst, handicapped at best, despite their hard work for their species' survival. Many of these individuals suicide, for despite their great sacrifice for the rest of us, they are unable to rejoin their species in any normal way.

Yes, we are interested in hiring members of several compatible species who do not have *pejiin,* to act as our tactical crews, to spare ourselves the destruction of these otherwise good Ayi men and women.

Any species would.

Yet we are looked down upon because we employ these people, whom we pay and support as our own. These non-Ayi individuals also are looked down upon by other species, and are called mercenaries, as though that is a curse.

We force no one to fight for us. We ask, or they volunteer. We pay, we support, and we honor those who choose to join us in this capacity.

We hope that eventually members of Humanity will be comfortable doing this, for we believe there is already a sympathetic relationship between our species and theirs. If they choose not to aid us in this way, we will think no less of them. We will not retaliate in any way, despite what some Compact members warn.

The Kynneth can do this job, but we have been reluctant to ask and train them for it, for two reasons. First, because their very innocence makes us look as though we are predatory upon them, this childlike species. To say they are good-natured, agreeable and social is to belittle them in the eyes of other species. To say they are perhaps less intellectually capable than others, may sound like judgement. But they are, all of that.

But the second reason is different.

They are, like many swift hunters, not capable of long periods of intense action. They are quick, but have little stamina.

They are fierce predators, having survived on a planet with thousands of species who tried to destroy them as they competed for living space, much as has happened on Earth. Humanity is considered less predatory than Kynneth, but rose from a similar abundance of enemies. But Humanity overcame their attackers. Kynneth are still struggling to do so on their home world.

We have removed many of them from those circumstances, as they have pleaded. We bring Kynneth to a planet that can support them in safety. They are free, there, to run and hunt and live without fear, with many prey animals and only a few predators. This action has the approval of Cuy.

Also, we have offered some Kynneth this choice, to fly with us and act as our defenders, and many of them accept.

We hope they will function well and will be as compatible as Humanity probably can be. But many other species in the Compact have looked at this relationship and judged it, and decided we have only freed them from certain death because, for our own selfish reasons, they can help us.

This is untrue.

We rescued them because they deserve to survive.

Ayi and Humanity are not in the same position, for Humanity have *freed* themselves *from competition to live*, and ultimately have outgrown their planet. They are strong and independent, and are imminently capable of refusing our offer should they choose to do so, or of accepting it—without the undeserved and harsh judgements of others.

To clarify, *pejiin* is *not* telepathy.

It cannot be used to influence another's decisions.

It is more akin to what some Humans call empathy. While it is a shared sense, like hearing, in that we all hear the same thing, in *pejiin* we all *feel* or sense the same thing.

It is not an active sense. In the same way that the sense of hearing cannot force someone else to change their mind, so too does *pejiin* only react. It is a passive sense. It cannot *do* anything.

Pejiin is much stronger when in the physical presence of another person, but it can still be felt between ships in normal space (though not if either or both of the two ships are in null).

Even if an enemy is targeted by unmanned, automated weapons systems, Ayi personnel will still sense any deaths as a result of those weapons' attacks—ours or theirs—to our detriment, unless we can protect ourselves with a *pejiin* screen.

Screening can help reduce the stress of sensing deaths in *pejiin,* like sound baffles in a room can prevent loud volume or echoing sound. Screens can prevent a whole ship or station of our people being affected.

Unfortunately such screening also reduces all the other sensors aboard the ship, visual and tactical, infrared and ultrasound, reducing our ability to dodge or to pinpoint targets. The result is that fighters cannot target at all *with* screening, so their weapon systems are useless in that case.

Rather than have all Ayi on a ship suffer, or, alternatively, permit that ship to be "blind" and unable defend itself, what we do is filter *pejiin* for the whole of the ship *except* for the tactical division.

Tactical may consist of only two or three persons who manage weapons in an "open" or unscreened portion of the ship, so they can accurately target and fire a response to any attack. They can only do this for a short period of time without the protective shielding a screen can provide.

Ultimately *pejiin will* transmit enough pain to disable a fighter. It *will* transfer the overwhelming fall into non-being of a badly injured or dying person. This will eventually send Ayi fighters into unconsciousness or death along with them.

Therefore, it should be obvious that we Ayi are not good at war.

This would be irrelevant if non-Compact species (and a few within the Compact) were not so determined to fight. They wish to acquire our ships, navigation data, and drives. Since these are our livelihood, we do not give them up easily.

They also attack colonies, both planetary and artificial stations, to acquire resources or more space for their overpopulated regions.

It is in our and the Compact's best interest for Ayi to be able to fight. Particularly House Dzarn which does most of the exploration and contact with other species.

We need to be able to defend ourselves. To accomplish this, we have welcomed individuals of other species onto our ships, to join our tactical crew.

The Kynneth are, in particular, eager to do this, for they have no starships of their own. We hope Humanity will join them, and us.

—Dzarn Reith Koras, of
Calindey's *Star Glow*

Chapter Seven: Sailing to War

Once more before we left, we were visited by Lady Calindey. Behind her and Reith came another of their people, carrying what looked like a plass box full of small black plass items from her shuttle.

"Thank you for coming to this meeting with such short notice," the ever-polite Lady Calindey said. I noticed our liaison Reith Koras, was staring at her. Something in the intensity of his gaze or the glimmer of adoration within it, told me the young man was in love with his lady.

It was sweet, and quite Humanly, so that I forgot for a moment that these were alien beings.

She nodded to Reith, who removed one of the items from within the box and held it up. He explained:

"This is what your people call a telephone or 'phone,' or 'comms.' It can contact any other phone on Azureign, by using the Compact satellites—the things you call spy eyes—that circle the planet above.

"These will help your Oracle group to remain in close contact with the Preserve flotilla so you can coordinate your attacks."

He then showed the Zeen and I—and Zola, who had arrived late—how to select one of the "available" phone numbers as our own, which we then "claimed" by adding our name next to that number.

Everyone with one of these "comms" could call everyone else on that list.

Each leader in Jiaru and several Priestesses were already listed, each with their own number. Besides these three main groups (that is, Jiaru, the Priestesses, and now us), the Ayi Lady Calindey and Reith were also listed, along with a few seemingly random Dragonriders, Rangers and representatives of other nations who had joined the revolt.

Reith showed us how to look up a person on the list and "call" them, and how to answer if someone called us.

Then he had us practice calling one another using our lists. When Zola called me, I felt a heavy vibration in my hand, and could hear it buzz. I answered and we both said "hello" and laughed at each other.

"This can be done for all your major people, and anyone else you think needs to be within instant reach of you, using the remaining numbers." He showed us about a half-dozen more of the small machines that remained in the box.

After we'd tried out a few more calls back and forth, he showed us volume control, and how to recharge them using small solar-panel units which they also provided.

"There is a way to display holograms so you can see the person you are talking to, but this uses much more energy, and would be obvious to the Compact members at the Oracle." Reith smiled. "But they will not notice the voice-only calls, so those are safe."

"Is this your technology?" Zola asked.

"No. These are from Earth," Reith explained. "They have been adapted so you can use them here with the Compact satellites."

He bit his lip and met our eyes, me, Mother and Zola one by one. "You do understand, you should not have access to any such thing, so it would be well to keep them hidden and on silent mode."

Zola and I nodded. Mother looked confused, so I stepped aside with her to show her the volume and silencing sliders that Reith had just shown me and then she nodded her understanding.

Then we went over the timing and using the phones to ensure we called the Ayi as well as our Oracle group when our fleet began to move.

We would call all the relevant people so we began our attack on the Oracle at the same exact time the flotilla began its attack on the Preserve, at the same time the Ayi blocked the spy-eyes. Until then, we were told, Lady Calindey's ship would hide our flotilla from view. The active spy-eyes would simply "not see" us.

Once the Oracle attack began their diversion, the Ayi would block the satellites entirely, so that no one else in the Compact would see our flotilla attack the Preserve, and—they hoped—they would prevent Oracle and Preserve from communicating with one another.

Reith had explained, "We cannot support this block for long, or we would do it now. It is more important they are blinded when the fight begins, so they cannot send help to the Preserve."

Besides shielding our flotilla from view, then blocking the satellites, the Ayi were also prepared to "drop protective shields" around us if there was any sign of military retaliation from the other Compact aliens, which they did not really expect.

Calindey then said something to Reith in their own fluid language, of which I picked out only one word: water. Reith turned to us.

"You have sufficient food and water for your people on your boats?"

"We think so, yes," I answered. "We have solar-powered desalination units on board every fifth or sixth ship, to refill our fresh water tanks."

"We can provide Earth-made high-energy travel foods, if those would be helpful."

My mother bit her bottom lip. After a moment of silence, she said, "It might be good to have such a thing, in case they are delayed by storms or other problems, for any length of time. If we don't need them, at least we will be easier of mind to know we have backup supplies."

Lady Calindey nodded a Human-type nod for "yes" and signaled to Reith. He walked up the ramp and into the ship.

While he was gone, she explained, "These foods were made for Humans on Earth. They have appropriate protein and vitamins and are packaged to be good for months or even years without spoiling. They are dry, though, so you will want extra water from your desalinators, and you will want to store them in a dry place."

When Reith reappeared on the ramp, he was carrying a box, and was followed by two more youths also carrying boxes. These they approached with and set on the table. Reith opened his box and held up a clear-wrapped rectangular packet about the size of one of our winter ginger cookies, though rectangular rather than round.

"They're wrapped with cellulose to stay dry and fresh," he said. He grinned his mischievous grin and said, "Of course, you aren't supposed to have these, either—"

"And we must keep them hidden," Zola finished. He nodded at her, still grinning. It seemed he found the whole notion of tricking the Compact aliens amusing.

"Reith will join you on the ships for the flotilla attack. If you like, I will assign another liaison for the Oracle attack group?"

Mother, Zola and I exchanged quick glances. It did not seem like a bad idea to me, but before I even said that, both Zola and the Zeen were nodding.

"Yes, thank you. I would feel better knowing there is one of your people to help get the timing and details right or if there is some complication we do not expect or comprehend."

Lady Calindey said some words to one of the two other young Ayi who had carried the boxes out. He (or she?) responded, also in their language, and the Lady looked satisfied.

"This is Vadi, who will remain here with Reith until you have the last balloons ready. Vadi will depart for the Oracle with your balloon group, while Reith goes with your boats, along with Zeden, I believe?"

Mother scowled. She was still trying to prevent me from going.

Meanwhile Calindey glanced at her two young people, then added, "You should know, if there is actual warfare in the sense of people being killed..." She looked flustered, the first time I'd seen her as anything less than confident and self-assured. She did not seem able to finish.

Reith took over. "She means to say that if there begin to be many deaths, then Vadi and I will need to be picked up to ride out the fight behind our *pejiin* screens on one of our ships." He blinked and glanced to me, Mother, and Zola. "We are not able to protect ourselves from...from feeling such things too much."

"We are being not much help to you, if we...fall down," Vadi said softly.

Calindey finished her warning. "Thus, I may need to return and pick them up once the attacks begin, depending upon how things go, but you will have their advice at least until then."

Clearly Vadi (whose gender we never did learn) did not speak Common nearly so well as Reith, as that short statement attested. but they all seemed to think Vadi's speech was good enough to be helpful with communications and coordination.

Reith had told me a little about their sense of empathy, and how it could be affected by death or the grave injury of others, whether ally or enemy. Ayi could not survive a war without their screens.

"I understand," I said, nodding, and all three of them seemed relieved.

My mother and sister were still confused. "I'll explain later," I murmured. Now was not the time, for I sensed—even without their sensing ability called *pejiin*—that it would embarrass our alien allies.

"Good luck, then," Lady Calindey said as she turned and retreated to her ship, leaving Reith and Vadi behind.

I hoped we would not need her good luck wish.

Mother continued to argue with me as departure day approached.

"Zola going to the Oracle is fine," she said. "But I will not endanger both of you."

"We cannot *lead our people* into this battle from here, mother. We bring the most ships, we provide the most sailors and supplies. Those all need leadership. We also have the balloons as our observation platforms that we must communicate and coordinate with. Not to mention the Dolphinfolk."

Her lips tightened, but I noticed she looked at the floor, not meeting my eyes. She knew I was right.

"Let me put it this way, mother. You the Zeen obviously cannot go, because someone must be left in power, here. Zola is going to the Oracle where she is needed to coordinate the balloon group.

"Kiké might be available, but no one else here besides me can communicate with the Dolphinfolk—at all, much less *well*. Since they are leading this attack and in fact the *entire revolt*—we must have someone there that can speak with them."

"I have a bad feeling," she murmured to the floor. "It is not safe."

"The Ayi have assured us repeatedly that they can shield us if there is need. But we expect no resistance from the Compact. We are simply destroying buildings, which are practically automated; the Lady Calindey checked for life signs at the Preserve. There are fewer than ten beings in the entire installation. And there are no weapons."

She still looked both dubious and stubborn.

"What are they going to do? Throw rocks at us?"

"I don't know. But if it was Tehassa's buildings you were attacking, I would fight back. How can we expect them not to?"

"The point remains, with what would they fight?"

"Those whips—"

"Won't reach far enough!"

She shook her head and walked away, but I knew I had won. I was going to the Preserve with the flotilla, just as I had planned all along.

Several days later, I boarded our flagship, called, simply, *Seashell*. Our accompanying fleet numbered more than sixty large vessels and even more smaller ones.

We went east, to the south end of Lynly, where we met up with all our allies.

Our flotilla is enormous, or so it seemed to me.

The Dolphinfolk steered us to the meet-point where we joined a few more ships from each of Azureign's nations, including even a pair from the Red, Queen Tae's enemy. There were also three from Vaimaey, our own pirate enemy. I hadn't expected that, but I guess the Dolphinfolks' cry for help has crossed the supercontinent and affected many of our people.

Our enemies were quiet, kept under close watch by sailors we trusted, and I have to admit, they behaved themselves admirably throughout.

What this says to me is that Humanity is as ready as the Dolphinfolk to free ourselves from the limitations of the Compact.

Our Tehassa contributed the most ships. But other places including Jiaru and Lynly added to our numbers—and most of them came well-armed with cannons mounted and prepared. I judged we had about two hundred fifty total smaller boats and ships gathered all together.

Along with sailing ships, many of them loaded with our Tehassan balloons, there were also many gymbal ball families, which dotted the water in clusters of red, blue, yellow, pink, orange and a few lavender or purple. They'd rigged up a system to keep their outer doors facing upward so they did not take on water, while their inner doors appeared to come to rest wherever the plant had grown them when the interior sphere was "right side up."

We still aren't certain why the Folk had asked for gymbals, although they seemed to think they would be useful for tending to the wounded, and as rest points for dragons; why our ships would not be available for those services was not explained.

Since the gymbals are not armed, they'd gather *behind* the ships once we reached the Preserve. Presumably they'd be out of range of any retaliatory weapons fire the aliens at the Preserve might bring to bear against our ships and various peoples, which, again, we absolutely did not expect.

The Ayi had suggested the other Compact members might not have weapons anywhere on Azureign at all, but no one actually *knew*. The Ayi had examined the Preserve with several types of sensors and found nothing.

The numbers of Dolphinfolk and whale allies in our flotilla were much harder to estimate, but there were many more than ships, of that I could be certain. The waters between our vessels teemed with pods of Folk. Around the edges of our massed fleet, I could see whale spouts and the bow waves the "big cousins" of the Dolphinfolk made, various types of whales cruising near the surface of the Ocean.

I did not see any of the eight-limbed "new friends" Split Fin had mentioned the last time we had met. These beings, members of the octopus family, I assumed, strictly lived underwater and did not breach to breathe. They had never encountered, much less communicated with Humans.

Split Fin suggested these octopoids would help pull things apart once the battle began, and might be helpful squirting their ink to hide the various ocean attackers. We would probably never see them.

Split Fin and Ingda both had said things which made me believe these new friends did not have even so much of a language as the whales did, certainly nothing as complex as the Folk used. Which made sense, because when had they needed to?

It did raise the issue of how they'd managed to explain their willingness to help to the Dolphinfolk. I just had to ignore that, since it was between the aquatic species, and nothing to do with us Dirt People.

Our ships and pods had met almost due south of Lynly's southernmost peninsula. We used our new comms to call Zola and the Oracle group and the Ayi ship led by Calindey. Our flotilla was ready to move.

Then we proceeded east toward our destination, across many kilometers of rough Azure Ocean.

Fittingly, pilot, gray, and Minke whales led the way. No one knew the exact distance by Human measurements, but we'd guessed we would reach our destination halfway around our world within roughly three tendays. The Dolphinfolk contributed to moving our ships and gymbals, often with more than one pod guiding and pushing each vessel along.

We also had good winds and spread our sails to carry us faster across the calmer-than-usual Ocean. Of course, sails weren't possible on the gymbals, so the Folk dutifully continued to push those, forming an arc around each one and pushing with their beaks or "shoulders."

So far during our gathering and sail, there had been no storms, major or minor. At night we could see the bright rings arching across the sky above, and in the dark spaces where the rings did not shine, we saw thousands of brilliant stars, the band of the Milky Way running through them like a wide, slow river.

Reith, who rode on the same ship I did, showed me the star of his home planet, an Ayi colony world named Koras Prime. His home city was the capitol of that world, where representatives of all Ayi Houses had home *keji,* that is, something like towns, ranging from city to village-sized. Each *kej* was composed only of members of that House. They lived together in compounds separated from the next House's *kej* with low but friendly walls.

Mostly friendly.

"Each House has a different set of beliefs, standards for life, and affiliations, where some Houses within a *kej* compound are allies, others are competitors or perhaps direct enemies," he explained.

Ayi don't war upon each other except via economic or political means. Kidnapping and more rarely, assassination are also used.

Some Houses have higher status than others, so the lesser Houses struggle to gain good alliances that help improve their status without bringing down their higher-ranked allies. Some become subordinate to a larger House for the greater economic protection this allows.

Now, out upon our ocean, Reith leaned against the polished wood rail of the Tehassan flag ship and stared at our assembly. It looked vast to me, but he muttered something about "not enough."

"What?" I asked him.

He bit his lip. "I have said Dzarn takes more risks than most other Houses," he began.

I nodded. "You are the galactic explorers of your species."

"And we trade with strangers." He quirked his mouth. "This makes us seem a little crazy to most of the other Ayi Houses, who prefer a more insulated life." He thrust his chin out at the flotilla that surrounded us. "I think we have never come so close to being "at war" before."

"You think they will fight back, at the Preserve," I said.

He nodded. "I also have decided that one or more of the Compact peoples here on Azureign, either at the Oracle or the Preserve, have been provoking you and your other colonists to get a reaction. Why, we are not certain."

I looked at him and saw his eyes were grave.

"I do not know how they usually behave on interdicted planets," I said, "but it does seem like they've broken their own Compact rules in several ways."

"Exactly," he said, tilted leaf-green eyes meeting mine again. "And I—none of us Ayi here—understand what that means."

I paused, suddenly swept by an atavistic urge to run away from him.

I can't decide if the Ayi looking so similar to us is worse or better than dealing with aliens that are just...totally *alien*. Like the slug-like Simbara, or the insectoid Mengsee race.

Ayi are too close, and yet are weirdly not close at all. It was as if I could feel from him the effects of millennia of explorations that I, poor dumb animal, could not encompass.

Reith had told me and my family about other even weirder aliens, such as Moradory, who apparently resemble huge soggy dumplings, that can extrude limbs and sensory apparati as needed from their bodies. The somewhat similar Abblak also look more like *things* than they do living intelligent beings.

Also there were the Asimsim, whom he'd compared to tall blue carrots with root-like tentacles used as manipulators and ambulatory limbs. And then there were the highly-advanced species called Sorasayn, who resembled walking trees with bad attitudes. Despite their surly and sarcastic demeanor, they actually like meeting and trading with new species.

I had been most excited to meet an actual Kynneth individual. He'd looked like an upright-walking, talking spotted cat with a prehensile tail. Many Kyn—also called Casakin, currently live aboard Ayi ships; they are in training to be pilots and other helpers to Dzarn.

In the Compact, the older species were *supposed* to act as mentors for the newer and younger species, such as Ayi did with Kynneth. I wondered who had done that for us.

Humanity is no longer considered a young species, having belonged to the Compact for well over a millennium by now, and having experienced contact with many other different peoples.

Of course, here on Azureign, Humanity had been interdicted. I and the others on our planet were a special case and we knew little about alien species, or even our own species from our home world. Our development had been so slowed, we were *less* advanced than our ancestors who had come here had been.

I wondered what the Ayi thought about us. I knew that sometimes I was fascinated by Reith and Calindey, while other times they just made me shudder, because they were so almost-but-not-quite-Human. A lizard-brain reaction, I'm sure, because they never have been unkind to anyone on Azureign so far as I know.

(Nor, Zola had reported, were they ever called unkind in any archives of the Library of Humanity by Humans who had met them long ago.) They were patient, helpful, and offered us valued guidance.

Being Human, I could not help but wonder what they wanted from us in return.

Meanwhile, they were helpfully blocking the Oracle's view of us by inserting fake footage into the Compact's satellite viewers so those showed empty ocean where our flotilla swam and sailed. I assume any sensors they might have at the Preserve would be likewise fooled by this method. Lady Calindey had promised we would remain unseen until we were ready to attack.

Although—what the Mengsee and Simbara and possibly the Toridani would do if they *did* see us coming was a moot point. Perhaps the blocking made no difference at all to what followed.

Chapter Eight: War Begins

Ingda's Whreng! Pod pushed the ship I was on, assisted by half of the members of a wild Ocean pod called Wavelift. The Folk could not rise to speak while they were pushing, but we had greeted one another when the flotilla first assembled and in between sessions of pushing. The Dolphinfolk now were free to push our boats or not, and at their own pace, dropping in or out to take a break from the work.

Despite what seemed to be chaos, all our ships and gymbals moved forward together, the Folk communicating and smoothly organizing shifts.

I climbed down the rope ladder on the side of our ship to be close to Ingda when she took a break.

"Are you ready to fight?" she asked before I could say anything.

"I believe so," I told her. "How are the Folk?"

She tail-danced, meaning "excited."

"Is there anything we can do to help you get us there?"

"The dragon is heavy," she said.

So they could tell when the beast was resting on the ship, versus flying up in the air.

"Should I tell Lon to have Quita rest on another ship sometimes?"

She porpoised alongside the ship for a few moments, presumably thinking about this. Then she said, "It will just make things hard for them, then."

"So, no?"

"No. It is good, we asked for their help. We did not expect dragons to be so fat. What are they eating?"

I was surprised she had not seen this for herself. "They eat fish, just like you do!"

"How do they catch fish? They cannot swim!"

"With their claws," I told her, surprised at her surprise.

She did a fin flap in the air, a shrug, and said, "There are plenty of fish." Then in an abrupt change of subject, she added, "We are halfway."

"Good," I said.

Beside her a Dolphinfolk I recognized as a member of Wavelift pod surfaced and slapped the water with a fin, meaning irritation.

"My turn to push!" Ingda called and dove out of sight.

The wild Folk person stared at me a moment then silently sank below the surface.

In stormy weather, or when the wind worked the waves up too high, the Dolphinfolk would need to wear a harness and swim in front of each boat, pulling it along as a group. It was slower, but still allowed them freedom to dive below the waves, then come up to breathe for a quick break before pulling again.

Now that we understood the Dolphinfolk were a people in their own right, it seemed demeaning for them to be harnessed as if they were simple-minded oxen or horses. But they wanted to be free of the Compact badly enough to subject themselves to it, to drag us to the Preserve as part of their fight for freedom.

It was a slow wet struggle to get the harnesses fitted onto them, whether we clung to the ladder and reached, or entered the water and tried to swim at the same time. As you might suppose they refused to keep them on when they weren't needed, so this process had to be repeated each time storm clouds showed up.

Several of the straps had broken the previous time we had had to put them on—and worse, it had been a false alarm, for no storm rose up making the whole effort unnecessary.

So I climbed back up the ladder and sat down with the harnesses that needed repair. It was tedious work, but better than doing nothing. Reith wandered over and sat down to help when he saw what I was doing. I suppose he was bored, as well.

Who would have thought going to a fight would be so boring?

A complication stirred things up: Before we even set out from Tehassa and unknown to me ahead of time, my little brother Kiké went with the Ayi.

He arranged with Reith Koras to go aboard one of Calindey's shuttles which carried him and two of his chairs to observe our battle from her big ship.

Later I learned he had been aboard *Star Glow* since shortly before we'd left Tehassa in our ocean-ships, to join the main flotilla off the tip of Lynly.

I had been so involved in the logistics, I'd not even noticed his absence. I'm certain my mother would have been apoplectic, if she'd known in advance. Kiké obviously snuck out.

Like the Kynnethi individual I'd met, the Ayi aboard the shuttle considered Kiké to be a sort of apprentice; they were tutoring him about their ship and House and how to fly their ship—and use their armaments.

I'd have worried much more if I'd known Kiké was doing that, which was no doubt why he'd not told me. I was also annoyed that Reith, our supposed ally, had kept this secret. But what could I say to this youth of powerful aliens? Did Lady Calindey know? She must. My brother was on her ship.

I found out when he called me.

I answered my comm and his voice, filled with laughter, rang out.

"Zeden! I can see you!"

"What?" I'm sure I sounded like the worst sort of *querfufu*, unable to process his simple statement. It's not like he said anything difficult, it's that it was so out of context it made absolutely no sense to me.

"What do you mean? How? Where are you?"

"I am on the *Star Glow!* Look up, way up into the sky!"

I did as he asked, and saw a dark speck high against the brightness of the rings. Presumably the Ayi ship.

"How— Why— What are you doing there?"

He laughed. He was so delighted, I could not chide him for this bit of escapism.

"They are showing me how the ship works!"

"Oh...that is good."

"Zeden, they have a waterfall! On a spaceship! Because it is their city, remember Reith told us about *kej*-ships? This is one, a whole city. And they wanted a fountain, so they built one! It's so beautiful." His laughter was contagious.

"Does Mother know where you are?" I wondered.

"Yes I just told her, and she told me to tell you. I think she is angry, or rather the Zeen is, but I don't care!"

I could hear that in his voice, that delight he claimed instead of a sense of fault that the Zeen would try to instill for this behavior.

I sort of grunted, to let him know I'd heard him.

"We can see how large your flotilla is—it's as big as all of Tehassa. Or that's how it looked when we rose above our home so I could see it. It's beautiful, too, but of course our Falls are much bigger—both wider and taller than the one here on *Star Glow*."

"Uh-huh," I said, thinking how little a view we get of Tehassa from a balloon. The highest I'd ever gone permitted me to see most of one single Isle. Did I envy him? Of course.

"I have a special camera and I am taking photographs, Zeden. I will show them all to you afterwards!" I laughed with him, and then he said, "Well, Deraff wants to go run simulations, so I will talk to you later."

"All right, Kiké, goodbye."

"'Bye!"

He was so excited, there was no way I couldn't feel happy for him.

Then I thought about our mother.

With me gone with the flotilla to the Preserve, my sister to the Oracle with the balloon group, and Kiké secretly aboard the Ayi ship, the situation was my mother's worst nightmare. All the heirs were outside of her protective zone. But maybe this was good for her, too. She would have to let us go sometime.

I knew my mother had sent an ambassador to the Oracle when we sent our first small group of "attack" balloons up there to the Lhasa Hills. She had strongly suggested to the Oracle personnel that a) It was time for the interdiction to end, and b) It was time the Compact changed its rules about war, since they were permitting *attacks* but not retaliations. Several nations' leadership had been badly damaged by this situation, ours among them, of course.

And wasn't one thousand years enough?

They had given her ambassador no response. Almost as if the woman hadn't contacted them nor said anything at all. She had gone through their Maze, which works kind of like an application for an appointment to visit the Oracle.

But when she got to the doors of the Oracle building, they ignored her request for a meeting. They ignored the documents my mother had sent with her ambassador. They acted as if our ambassador wasn't even there. To say they ignored us doesn't encompass the completeness of their disregard. It was as if we are invisible.

It was not the first time we had been treated thus. They had ignored the murder of my father and the attack on my brother, not to mention all of what the Red had done to Jia and Maladh.

It almost seemed as if they *wanted* us to break with the Compact; as if they were *goading* us to war, as Reith had intimated.

It has become clear to us that the Compact representatives on Azureign poorly understand the Human need for independence. And they see our simultaneous desire to belong to a group as a paradox.

We want to do our own thing, but we also want to belong to a group of our own kind, that has similar beliefs, or at least is tolerant of *other* beliefs. We're neither herd animals like the Chondor and Ayi, nor completely individualistic like the Deesangua and to some degree the various Mengsee species.

This apparently confuses them. Or at least the Mengsee, Simbara and Toridani. I think the Ayi have begun to understand.

We of Tehassa and Jiaru—and our enemies—agree that we should be allowed to fight each other if we wish to, to settle things between us. To be attacked, but not be permitted to retaliate doesn't make sense to us.

"So, I have a question," I asked Reith. He turned to me. "Is this considered immature behavior, this attack of ours? Does the Matrix chart have a special column for people who go to war?"

Reith looked at me with a small smile on his face. "Even citizens of the universe that the Matrix has classified as *advanced* have conflicts not so different from this," he said. "We Ayi have been attacked repeatedly by vicious aliens called Kimi. And we defend ourselves as best we can. Is it war?" He shrugged. "So war is a thing I think will never go away. And to answer your question, yes there is a column for describing how aggressive each species is."

"And Humanity is on it, no doubt."

"You are about average. You do not usually attack unless provoked; you will defend yourselves if at all possible. But, you are willing to compromise to bring fighting to a conclusion, which Kimi are not, for example."

We stood at the rail and watched the waves and other ships, the Folk rising to breathe and diving again.

"The Matrix of Ascension is a Cuy creation. We Ayi also have come to believe that it is a valid descriptor of the various known species." He glanced at me, mouth quirked. "There is supposedly a species that exists somewhere in the galaxy or the universe, that fills each cell of the Matrix. It's a way to think of the kinds of beings that exist and how they might grow and change." He used his fingers to brush back his hair from where it had blown into his eyes.

"It's like a growth chart?"

"The Cuy believe that at some point in time, each species will rise in the Matrix to become more Cuy-like. *More sane. More advanced.*" He laughed. "This is an over-simplification, as you might imagine. The Cuy are complicated, as are their beliefs. They are exceedingly old."

The Matrix was difficult for me to get my head around. It was a belief system almost like a universal religion in its tenets—so far as I understood them.

I think the important thing to remember is this: The Cuy observed thousands of species across many thousands—perhaps even millions—of years. Those observations, the history of the universe's living beings, all contributed to the creation of their Matrix.

The Matrix is fairly irrelevant to us as we sail our ships east, but it is something to think about.

Likewise, something to think about was the Queen of Pirates, who had once been Princess Tae of Jia.

When the Pirate Queen Tae and I had been introduced, we were somewhat wary of one another. We had ended up choosing our mutual war preparations as a sort of neutral topic we could discuss without awkwardness.

While her fluency in the Folk language was at least as good as mine—perhaps better—her understanding of physics, in particular the dynamics of the planned battle, was weak.

We spent awhile discussing sonics, during which time I tried as gently as possible to improve her understanding of what the whales were going to do. Of course I mentioned the old example of a singer finding the correct *resonant frequency* of a glass. This could be any particular musical note. After matching that note and singing it, vibrations can shake the glass apart. This she had heard about and understood.

I cannot say I was strongly taken with the Queen, but as her feelings seemed to be the same, we parted in a cool, friendly manner, and our Dragonrider took her back to her ship.

I was much more concerned about the battle to come and everyone's part in it than I was about possible marriage partners.

We might not even survive this, after all.

By building their research center—or whatever it was—at the Preserve, the Compact aliens had not only broken their own rules, but had destroyed the previously untouched wildlife that we assumed lived there.

All we knew about the Preserve was that it was "small." But small compared to what? We also had no idea how big the settlement upon the Preserve was, if it just included a few buildings, or if it was what we'd consider a city.

We would see soon enough, but I have to say there wasn't much to do aboard the ship while we sailed for tendays, so speculation was rife.

I'd read all the book cubes I'd brought—some of them more than once. Zola had brought some cubes from the Library that had photographs taken all around Earth. While beautiful, they did not mean much to me. I'd rather have seen such photographs of Azureign, that I could relate to more.

I'd talked with the other sailors, fighters, and Dragonriders aboard until I felt like I knew every facet of them and their families, and some on other ships, as well.

Lon Diderot and his dragon rode aboard our flagship. As did Gabriel Zev, an ally of the Jiaru "pirates," who was in charge of the Human portion of the attack group. I'd learned more about them than I probably wanted to.

I was glad I had been relieved of the responsibility to run the fight, since I knew nothing about how to organize ships *or* a battle. I could organize supplies, meeting space, and other logistics. But to assign ship disposition and arrange the naval tactics? Those were things Zev had done at least once before, while I had never contemplated it.

Instead, I organized things, like a break, where the Dolphinfolk swam away, leaving our ships paused on the ocean, while everyone swept their decks clean of the various animal poop, which we did not want to risk dropping onto our Folk friends. Exciting, no?

Over half our food animals had been fed to either the dragons or ourselves, as a break from fish. I'd taken a definite dislike to Sable Fish, since we'd had the buttery things three or four days out of each of the first two tendays. Normally, they're a treat, but not when you're stuck with them. Somehow, they'd become the easiest things to catch. Broiled, baked, stewed, gumboed, and steamed. I'd ended up only eating my potato the previous night, because it was Sable Fish again, grilled to perfection, and yet not even *smelling* attractive to me, even with chives and lemon on it.

We had anisa algae and Benqi fruit coming out our ears, too, but fortunately those still appealed to me.

The Dolphinfolk traded off their active pods at night, and now we were being assisted by a big pod I'd never heard of before. The Whreng! Dolphinfolk hadn't even introduced us to this new group. All I knew of them was that they kept our flagship at the "front" of the flotilla, slightly ahead of all other ships, and in front of the rest of the Dolphinfolk and their big cousins which surrounded and intertwined with our ships and pods.

So we were the first to see the ominous clouds on the horizon, that piled up and up, blotting out the rings and the sky above. Each ship that saw that storm warning rang their bells, alerting crews and passengers that things were about to get rougher.

Blazes of lightning lit up the area red all around us, followed eventually by thunder that got closer and closer. The wind picked up, and then the waves got higher and more violent, tossing our ships and gymbals like toys.

That night was miserable. I was extremely glad I had not eaten any of the rich Sable Fish.

The next morning, the sun rose all innocent and bright, and it was as if nothing had ever happened, all traces of the storm were gone except for a few puddles on the deck.

We lost one ship—one of the Corrigan refits, which kind of made sense to me; those had not been built to survive on the Ocean, and our simple upgrades had not been enough to make it seaworthy. Or I suppose I should say "ocean-worthy," because it would have been fine if still on the Inner Sea, which has much milder storms. Practically none, by comparison.

We picked up five sailors from that wreck onto various ships. That was about half the crew that had been on it. Ordinarily such rescue would have seemed a miracle, except each ship had been *surrounded* by Dolphinfolk, so there were plenty of good swimmers to help the survivors aboard nearby ships.

I knew personally none of the people that had been lost, but that did nothing to change the somber attitude of our own crew and passengers. Our first deaths. I could see Reith was uneasy, but he said nothing.

After nearly three tendays, always heading due east, we saw a black shadow rise on the horizon. Almost as if a pointy black sun was rising.

It got taller and bigger, and finally we could see that it was an enormous volcanic mountain, surrounded by a rim of relatively flat land, its old and cooled previous lava flows. On the northern edge of that flat land were a cluster of strangely-shaped buildings.

I have to say, the Preserve was a disappointment to me. I thought I would be seeing unusual trees and flowers and animals. Instead, the Isle was black and brown and grey rock. I saw a few scraggly shrubs, but no trees. Through the binoculars, we could make out a few places where simple grasses eked out a living in the cracks of the cooled lava. So, we were wrong to accuse the aliens of destroying any native life on the Preserve. There wasn't any. There might never have been. The volcano had already taken care of that.

The buildings the aliens had constructed almost looked like a natural part of the island Preserve, matching the background in their stony greyness. One alien tower stuck up, shining like it might have been made from obsidian.

We had reached our target, but we thus saw few signs of life.

Whiyira rose from the Ocean and chittered. Mosi, the lead whale, rose beside him and spouted. It was time.

I used the phone given to us by Calindey to call Zola with the Oracle group, to put them on alert. Our attack was beginning. They should begin also.

As planned by the Dolphinfolk and whales, the first wave of the attack was literally gigantic waves created by all the whales combined. This was accomplished by the whales only.

The whales swam in patterns, pushing bow waves before them that combined with the natural Ocean waves and magnified them. A low, slow tsunami rose among the buildings, swamping some of the lower ones entirely.

While the whales built their attack, the Dolphinfolk appeared to play. There was a lot of chittering, tail-dancing and whistles of excitement. I'd guess they were building up their energy, rather like a General giving an uplifting speech to their troops.

There were no seawalls or other protections built by the aliens that might have protected them from the waves. Perhaps they didn't care if those low buildings were flooded--there was no way for us to tell.

There was certainly no *reaction* to the water that flooded further and further inland. We saw no personnel. We saw no automated systems doing anything to protect the installation.

Either there was no one there to notice, or the Compact aliens were doing what they had previously done: They ignored us.

The Folk and their cousins spent a few moments preparing their sonic attack. I heard nothing at first, nor could we see any effect.

We had half-expected this from their earlier demonstrations.

After a few minutes the water seemed to shimmy, and even through the natural waves around our ships we could see vibrations making the water tremble.

After a time, these vibrations became obvious on the land, as the singers "tuned up." We saw some of the buildings and the rocks they were built upon vibrate. I had assumed they would find the note for each particular building, destroying them one at a time. Then I thought they'd use the earth shake to take down the rest, the ones they could not find the resonant frequency for, but instead, both those things seemed to be happening at once.

I could feel the core-deep rumble of sound that we get when an earth shake begins.

I could see various buildings crack and fall apart. Dust rose in a haze obscuring some of what was destroyed while the whales and Folk sang.

Chapter Nine: Oracle and Preserve

Meanwhile, Zola and our balloon crews set about their program to distract the aliens at the Oracle site.

Her report, which I saw and heard later, went as follows:

As expected the screen dome over the Oracle repelled the Dragonriders, but our balloons went through it as if it wasn't even there. Soon there were over a dozen balloons clustered over the site, which included the Maze, the stele and its beacon, and a half-dozen buildings, all visible but slightly fuzzy beneath their dome-like shield.

When Zeden called to begin our fight, I (Zola) signaled the others, who ignited their bombs and dropped them. Each of the thirty or so balloons that could be safely deployed over the dome dropped ten or twelve of the grenade-type bombs, many of which hit and exploded at close to the same time in the first wave; the second and third were more erratically timed.

We saw the shield fail. The warped light disappeared beneath us and the Oracle buildings seemed to snap into sharp focus. This was as unexpected as it was welcome.

Then our Dragonriders joined in, dropping rocks and nudging or dragging balloons back over their targets, while the balloon crews dropped the rest of our bombs. These weapons did little to actually damage the facilities, but the bombard did have the effect of kicking a termite mound.

Aliens swarmed from the buildings, staring up at the sky in apparent astonishment.

As soon as these people appeared, we stopped dropping things. Our job was not to injure anyone, but to keep them busy so they could not discover the interference with nor repair their satellites.

Our plan was that this would buy time for our forces at the Preserve to keep attacking, where we did not care so much if we injured or killed anyone—mostly because the

Dolphinfolk were so angry. But where the primary goal at the Preserve was destruction, ours at the Oracle was diversion, which we accomplished.

The other limit on our attack, of course, was the balloons themselves. They do not tend to stay in one place. While the Dragonriders could pull or push them back over their target, there were many more balloons than dragons, and eventually the airships drifted away from the site on the prevailing winds.

Once our Dragonriders had the aliens' attention, some of them moved to places where there were no alien people swarming around, and continued to drop rocks.

This elicited shouts and anger from the Oracle personnel, who had probably never imagined that we on Azureign could or would do such a thing, I suppose.

To be honest, it was difficult for our crews to not collapse in laughter, because of the great astonishment and helplessness of the Oracle aliens we could see swarming around. The Oracle personnel did nothing at this point to fight back, which is what we had all expected.

Eventually, the Oracle got their shield back up, and all their people went back inside, and so the other half of our balloon group pulled up anchor and began a second attack wave. The dragons pulled the balloons into attack formation above the shield dome and more bombs were dropped.

Most of the first balloon group sailed off into the grasslands of Lhasa, but my ship stayed behind to observe and offer suggestions. We tethered our craft to a tree, which worked to hold it in place for a while.

The other half of the balloon crews lit and dropped their bombs until the shield failed again, and again the people ran out, shouting and pointing.

This time it was not so funny.

The aliens brought weapons with them. They had the sparking whips we already knew about from our previous experiences with them. The whips were long *enough to reach and snap around the feet—and in one case, the wing—of the lower-flying dragons.*

Dragons roared in pain, and flew up, dragging the more stupid of the Oracle people with them, because they could not or would not relinquish their grips on their nasty whips.

I could see the Dragonriders use knives to cut the whips loose, which incidentally injured them as well as their dragons, zapping them as they used those metal tools to free their flying mounts from the whips. The remnant whips dropped to the ground along with any persons still clinging to them, and several aliens were injured and one apparently died, this way, still holding on to their stupid whip. Were those things so rare and expensive that they refused to sacrifice them?

There was a new kind of weapon, in addition to the whips.

These were a kind of fat rifle that fired globs of exceedingly hot, flaming material, and these began doing serious damage to both dragons and balloons, to my horror.

I instructed my people to light and drop the rest of their bombs all at once, and then move out of range, as the dragons had now done.

"Sail free," I told them.

The fire-guns were more than we had bargained for.

One balloon caught fire, the envelope going up with a whoosh. The basket crashed into the ground, and its people did not get out. Dead? Injured too badly to move? Or merely stunned?

I could not tell, as by then, the top of the tree my balloon's drag rope had been tethered to stripped off, releasing our little airship. The basket and envelope went spinning off uncomfortably. As it spun, I was able to glimpse the ground, to see the various injured and dead below.

And closer, I saw also the effects of the injuries and the death had had upon Vadi, the young Ayi youth who had joined us to help with communications and tactics. He was curled into himself in a corner of the basket of our balloon, like a child in the throes of nightmare.

"Can I help you somehow?" I asked him.

"I am already calling for a lander to pick me up," he told me in a small gasping voice. "It is being here soon."

And indeed, before he even finished speaking, I heard the swish of a small Ayi teardrop ship's arrival.

Rather than asking us to land the balloon, which would then have had to be refueled before it could rise again, the Ayi ship extruded a ramp with a sort of "hand" on it that gripped the edge of our basket, stopping the spin of the balloon and linking our two vehicles together. We held that delicate position for a moment while Vadi scrambled up the ramp and into the Ayi ship. Then the ramp and ship disappeared and the air whooped into that space.

"What?" one of the balloonists asked me.

"We knew that might happen," I explained. I pointed behind us to the ground, where the dead green alien lay, his whip strands visible along with deep blue burns across its body, where it had injured its own self as it fell.

I did not feel sad or even responsible for that death, but it did affect Vadi, no matter who had caused it.

"The Ayi sensory systems can feel the pain and deaths of others. Vadi was overwhelmed and needed to get to their ship, which is screened somewhat against this kind of reaction."

"Huh." The man then pointed to the ground, where we could see Oracle personnel still swarming around, most holding some kind of weapon. "What do we do now?"

"Well, our job was to distract them, and that is what we have done. So...we keep at it while we can."

But that would not be long, as our balloon drifted to the edge of the cleared area around the Oracle station.

"I hope the Dragonriders are okay," one of our crew said.

I could see that a number of them were missing from the sky.

"Probably gone to aid their dragons' injuries," I said. "I think even if they all had to leave, we've done plenty."

He grunted, looking around at the sky and then the ground below. The Oracle people were starting to return inside.

I took the opportunity to drop the last few of our bombs over a tiny Oracle out-building, which did virtually no damage. Then we let the wind carry us away.

Thus was Zola's report. At that time, she called me to let us know the diversion at the Oracle was finished. They had done all they could do.

I reassured my sister that the attack here was progressing as expected, as it had been—at that time.

The whales apparently found the note, or rather the frequency, for the ground around the buildings.

Unlike normal earthshakes, this one did not fade, nor did it come to an abrupt halt. It continued, on and on.

The roar was hellish.

Despite the Folk's reassurance that the sonics would not affect us, I saw many people on our ships fall to their knees or stand and hold their heads.

Then, bizarre as it seems in retrospect, we made a serendipitous discovery.

We had run out of hammocks and sleeping mats for some last minute crew added to our ships. To help give them a place to sleep, we'd raided every room of the palace for carpet or throw-rugs, including some of the otherwise useless Chem-O-Color rugs. All these we used for sleeping mats.

The Chem-O-Color rugs are completely frivolous. I had wished many times we had been given other things, more *useful* things by the Oracle, instead of rugs that would change color. And that had to be "fed."

So Chem-O-Color rugs did not hold much favor in our palace, often finding their way into unused guest rooms where they would go grey from lack of feeding. Or they were stuffed into boxes and sent into storage. Despite their uselessness at home, they were thick enough to provide a mattress-type bed on the decking of our ships, irrespective of their color-changing abilities.

But now, we discovered as some of the crew pulled the rugs over their heads, trying to deaden the sound, that the rugs were excellent at blocking sound! I saw such relief on the faces of those who had pulled a Chem rug over them that I tried it myself.

What a difference! Who would have thought?

We finally found a use for the stupid things.

And later we did not even chide the Folk or their big cousins for the overflow of sound. They did not have Human ears or Human heads; they did not know how and how much their sonics might affect us. They could have aimed and concentrated their sound waves to go across the Preserve all they liked, and still we would be affected because sound goes everywhere and Human ears are more sensitive than they understood.

So we thanked the Oracle for giving us these rugs which we now put to an entirely different use than they had imagined. I went below and dug out the rest of the ones on our ship and passed them around. I called Captain Bibi who rode on another ship. I managed, through the wall of sound the phone could filter out only some of, to tell him about the rugs.

Surprising me, the waters beneath our ships did not rough up during the sonic attack. I could see the shiver that meant sound waves were perturbing the sea waves. But that changed when the swell of the early tsunami waves finally receded back toward us. I feared the result of that returning swell.

Would our ships be pushed away from the isle? Would the fading waves shove us onto land and smash our ships?

I did not have much time to worry about that. Whiyira, leader of all the Folk, rose from the rolling waters and signaled our cannons to shoot. The cannoneers lit fuses, every barrel of our cannons pointed at the land, half of them lit at a time.

Then they went off, almost simultaneously.

The noise was astonishing. It was followed promptly by the other half of the cannons, our second barrage, going off.

We saw no people on the island, only buildings. Only those buildings falling apart.

There was an abrupt silence as the whales took a break from their sonic attack and all the cannon crews reloaded. This gave the dust and water time to settle a bit, so we could see our results.

Ocean water heaved among some stubs of buildings. A dome I had seen when we arrived now looked like a broken eggshell; equipment or blocky somethings inside it were flooded and being carried around by swirling waves. Things had broken loose and bobbed or sank. There was an eerie shrill squeaking noise as components of the various buildings, now visible, continued to shake and break.

It seemed to me that like a bell ringing, vibrations from the sonics continued to reverberate, and thus continued to shake things apart. Or maybe the earth shake was continuing; I had become partially deaf and insulated against the noise so I had trouble identifying sounds.

I don't know how many whales participated. More than there were ships, I think.

I saw the whales gather in the ocean between us and the isle. Their moaning songs began to come together again into one big wailing note, as they tuned up.

Then they held the single note they had found, and again the deep earth shake rumbling began. The whales then moved aside and Whiyira rose from the water and directed the next round of cannon fire to proceed from all our ships.

This time the vibrations died down more swiftly, and we could both see and hear our cannonballs strike rock and plass. Both natural stone and artificial constructions cracked or shattered, stone splinters flying briefly above the water.

Then there was silence.

The whales took a break from their efforts. The Folk assessed what was left of the Preserve while we Dirt People looked over our flotilla.

We had some ships capsize, mostly those that were not regular Ocean vessels, plus a few that had been what I assumed were badly-balanced ships: they went over and sank so fast. These tipped just enough for a high wave to flow over them, so they began taking on water faster than they could pump it out. Then—all the way over they went, capsized and sinking rapidly.

Many Dolphinfolk came and supported survivors who were injured or poor swimmers. These they guided to the gymbal pods, where the people inside unbalanced their balls enough to put their doors near water level. The injured then climbed or were push/pulled aboard. I noticed one gymbal, which had taken on seven or eight people, being nudged outside the flotilla by a few of the Folk. Getting the injured out of the fight.

Those people who were uninjured, or who were good swimmers, made their way to other ships and climbed up ladders, going onboard to reinforce the crew on those ships.

There were a few Folk injuries, and one whale, which had somehow acquired a bloody scrape just below its dorsal fin. I couldn't imagine how we could treat a whale, but fortunately, the medic did.

The whale swam to a particular gymbal, and the Human medic aboard calmly tipped their gymbal ball to make the outer door accessible. She then exited carrying a bag, and walked onto the whale's back, then along its side as it rolled gently, exposing the wound. There the medic knelt and proceeded to treat the scrape, mostly with simple herb packs, which stopped the bleeding, and then a cleanse. Via some signal inobvious to me, that seemed sufficient to both her and the whale, and the medic climbed back into her gymbal, which had been moved back beside the whale again by a Folk pod.

The whale swam, spouted, dived and disappeared beneath the choppy waves while the gymbal was restored to its original position.

I am still uncertain why the Folk decided gymbals are better than a ship or small boats for this service, but they did seem to work. Perhaps because the gymbal balls could not be armed, they were a more neutral vessel than our ships, which all carried cannons or fighter air ships. Maybe the Folk did not conceive of a hospital ship; we never learned why the gymbals were preferred.

The balloons were working as spotters for injured Folk and Humans in the water that needed help. Each balloon had to be tethered to a ship so they would stay in place, which turned out to be a nuisance for navigation. I think the Folk had imagined we were better at this than we are, having never practiced such a thing.

I called back half the balloons, which were deflated and pulled back onto their ships' decks, which simplified things a little. The remaining balloonists could still see enough of the water to pick out people who needed help, but their tethers were now far enough apart not to tangle, and there was more room for our ships to maneuver without knotting up.

Thus we collected ourselves during that pause in the attack.

But that peace, that silence, was not nearly the end of it. To say that things went beyond our control would be to hugely minimize the events that followed.

Reith murmured beside me, his face pale and set in a deep wince of pain. Then abruptly there was a whoosh beside us, within the swirly bubble shield-dome. One of Calindey's small "shuttles" popped into being from nowhere, like they do.

Reith turned to me and bowed. "I must leave for safety behind the *pejiin* screen," he said. "My people will protect you. We apologize for the loss of your ships and people, the waves are stronger and more unpredictable than expected."

I watched him slump aboard the shuttle, wishing I could go with him. I was tired, wet and cold. But we weren't done yet.

Even as I wondered if there was anything left of the buildings beneath the waves over the isle, I felt/heard the rumbling of the sonics again as the remaining whales and Folk began another attack and earth shake.

Then came real drama, unexpected, and world's-end violent.

I don't know if it was intended or not, but the sonic attacks had shifted something deep within the isle. The volcano that was the foundation of the Preserve came abruptly alive.

There was a stunning, mind-numbing, ear-killing explosion.

Even the whales stopped swimming, stunned.

I could see Folk rising from the water to shake their heads, as if they could clear from their ears that astonishing blast.

I, myself, could hear nothing. It was like watching a holocube with the sound turned off.

The volcano belched clouds of filthy dark ash that mostly hid from view the dangerous spray of deep red lava that spattered up into the sky above the cone. And came down everywhere around us.

It was as if Azureign herself had smashed a giant fist down upon us all, to stop the fighting, or so I imagined.

Calindey's shield prevented some of the damage we might have taken, but not all.

With the earth shake and volcanic explosion, waves were generated that *did* hit us, pushing all our vehicles away from the Isle. However well Calindey's shield worked, many of us were now no longer beneath its safety.

I saw several ships catch fire as flaming bombs ejected by the volcano hit them, one large enough to crack the back of the unfortunate ship it landed on.

As my hearing gradually came back, muffled by what I would later learn was damage to my eardrums, I could hear the volcano's roar.

The few dragons and their riders that had been in the sky, flew slowly in through the shield and took refuge on the bigger ships.

Of course, all the remaining balloons we'd had up were either destroyed or rapidly pulled inside the shield, then deflated and taken apart. The sky was no longer safe.

With each disastrous moment of the fight and then the volcano, we lost a few more people and ships, and even a couple gymbals.

We soon had more refugees than we could handle on our remaining ships.

I noticed Calindey's people had adjusted the shield so that it covered us all once again, even as we helped survivors from the water. I saw lava bombs hit the shield and slide down into the ocean, hissing and sometimes exploding as they touched the cold water.

"Thank the heavens for that shield," our Captain muttered as he wrapped a sailor in a blanket.

"We should move away," I suggested. "We hadn't counted on a volcano."

The Captain's jaw moved as he looked beyond our ship's rails to the water, to the wounded and floundering ships and people. "We have to pick up survivors first," he said.

Just don't say, *things could be worse,* I silently asked him. Thankfully, he did not say anything more.

But things got worse anyway. Much, much more, impossibly worse. As if a surprise volcanic eruption wasn't enough.

INTERVAL: Enemy Action

Like any Ayi, I was sad and embarrassed to leave the battle. Too many deaths among the sailors threatened to overwhelm me. Nausea roiled in my stomach. My head felt like someone had hit it with granite boulders.

I headed back aboard the *Star Glow,* where I could be safe from the powerful effects of people dying. Injuries we can usually withstand, but not deaths. The more sensitive in *pejiin* the individual is, the more strongly they are affected when people are hurt or killed.

Besides the nausea, and probably helping to cause it, my eyes had lost their ability to focus, zooming in and out without control.

But far worse was the swift black tunnel that pulled at me in *pejiin* with each person—both Human and Folk—who died. Even creatures we consider to be "only animals" can affect us this way. I felt a whale die, and it hurt; the whale's fellows were sad and felt the loss, and I felt their pain as well. That death, however, did not draw me into the death tunnel.

To me, this marks the difference between animal and person.

If I had remained with the flotilla on Azureign...the death tunnel would have pulled me in. Then it might have pulled me *beyond,* to the white light that can be seen at the end of that dark, racing tunnel.

And then I would be dead, too.

The more of us that are affected, the more the effect builds in *pejiin.* A feedback loop like that can destroy an entire Ayi city. Alone we are vulnerable, but in a group—without a screen to protect us—we could end up drawing each other into death.

It hurt, though, to leave the Humans and Folk to manage on their own. I felt I abandoned them when they needed help most. Just when I could, perhaps, have offered useful suggestions, I required rescue. Like some weak coward.

Now aboard *Star Glow,* safe behind our *pejiin* screen, I watched the battle progress while my eyes slowly returned to normal.

Humanity has a saying: *I sat on my hands.* Thus I was, helpless to do anything except perhaps make matters worse by adding my own distress to the general *pejiin* field.

Kiké, at least, welcomed me back, along with Derraff, our Kynnethi trainee. They seemed happy together. It was *good* to see them, a considerable emotional shift for me. I went from death tunnels to this: Apparently, in my absence, Derraff and Kiké had become friends.

They spoke together in quiet conversation, the Kynneth's soft purry voice complementing Kiké's accented ancient-Earth-Common burr. After listening closely, I realized Kiké also had adopted some Kynnethi words, along with some of our Ayi Trade language terms, so their conversation was a polyglot, which they both seemed to understand quite well.

I listened to them as a way to help distance myself from what we could see happening, below.

I seated myself behind the *pejiin* screen edge, of course, but not so far from the two young aliens that I could not hear them. Kiké in his rolling chair, Derraff on a cushion on the floor, both looking very much like they belonged there.

Beside me, Lady Calindey sat in her command chair, eyes on the screens in front of us. In addition, smaller screens repeating drone images were on pads attached around her chair.

Me, she ignored, almost as if I had done something wrong. Even though I knew she merely focused on what was occurring, with no time for me, her back-turned attitude added to my guilt. Vadi had rejoined the ship just before I did, and was seated among other young people of our *kej*. He and I exchanged a single, pained glance, and then ignored one another.

We had placed many drones above the flotilla which transmitted a panoramic view of events to our screens. We could observe the Dolphinfolk and Human efforts against the Mengsee and Simbara installation.

I do not add Toridani to that alliance against the Azureign settlers, though we still did not know what their stance was, in this. Not for certain. They will communicate only with Cuy, so to us their actions and thoughts are always mysterious. I did not see any of their peculiar spiky buildings amongst those at the Preserve. Thus, it did not seem Toridani had been an active participant in these interdiction-breaking activities.

I also did not know what part Toridani had played in general, in their role as interdiction observers. Unlike Mengsee and Simbara, Toridani are not gregarious. Unlike Mengsee and Simbara, they only had two or three individuals placed at the Oracle. So it would seem their influence was as small as their presence, on Azureign.

The flotilla, and in particular Humanity's whale allies, were making progress in their determined effort to flatten the buildings at the Preserve, despite losing the help of boat after boatload of sailors, cannoneers, balloon people, and even gymbals and a single dragon, (which they later managed to rescue from the sea).

The waves may have been directional, but they roughened the ocean. Meanwhile the Folk were busy adding sonics and were not Helping keep the ships bow-on to the waves. The whale and Folk allies were having a tough time of it.

The attack proceeded by alternating series of water waves, sonic waves, and cannon bombardment.

The combined whale and Dolphinfolk earth-shaking sonics worked perhaps a bit too well. They did shake the foundations, toppling buildings, so that there wasn't much left of the installation at the Preserve.

But also, they awakened the volcano that comprised the foundation of the isle.

We'd assessed the geophysics of the Preserve isle as soon as we had learned how the allies had planned to destroy the buildings. We had judged that those various species on Azureign did not have sufficient acoustic power to affect the dormant volcano.

We actually had not even been certain they could generate a seismic event, that is, that their sonics would be able to create earth shakes strong enough to bring down buildings.

We did not even begin to imagine they could crack open the volcano.

In this, we were dangerously wrong.

The whales and Folk created earth shake after earth shake, the tremors finally breaking down the blockage that had kept the lava contained, so the caldera walls were weakened and the molten rock was unleashed. Essentially, they shook out the plug on the lava vent.

Then, as you might expect, the volcano erupted.

Things became completely unpredictable on the ground and ocean at this point.

The only good news was that despite the terrible power of the volcano, there was no pyroclastic flow.

If there had been, I do not think even our shields would have been enough to protect the flotilla from the superheated ash and rock flow of such an event. So we were lucky that did not happen.

Other things did. Unexpected, passionate, brutal and terrifying things.

I was lucky I was already gone, for there were many deaths.

Even from up here, things were bad enough.

Three Ayi youths were at the unscreened tactical controls area of *Star Glow*, keeping our position steady, adjusting the shields as needed, and monitoring the many drones.

When the volcano blew, these three gasped in pain. One threw himself from his seat and crawled toward us. Toward the *pejiin* screen.

A second, this one a young woman, slumped over her control panel, apparently lifeless.

The third gasped again and leaned over his boards hands poised, teeth clenched, as he tried to brave it out. Because suddenly there were tens of deaths. These losses beat against the *pejiin* screen, threatening to pull us all in.

Calindey immediately ordered shield after shield placed over the flotilla, stretching *Star Glow's* power to the limits. It was too late for some Humans and Folk, but many remained, and our shields would help.

I leaped from my chair and pulled the crawling boy from the unscreened tactical area into safety. One of the others seated by Calindey dared the open-*pejiin* section to run in and grab the young woman, who looked dead to me. They got her behind the screen, but she remained unmoving.

The third was able to get the extra shields up and ejected another set of drones, then he, too, had to dive behind the pejiin screen.

The only ones now anywhere near the controls were Kiké and Deraff.

But that was only the beginning of the rebels' problems.

Abruptly in the smoky sky, hundreds of stone-chunk-rectangular ships appeared above the flotilla. Mengsee.

The ships rained fire down on the essentially unarmed fleet, because what good were antique cannons against Mengsee spaceships and their plasma guns?

Certainly the Folk had no armaments nor defense against this fire from the advanced starships.

The Mengsee plasma fire continued unabated, with no response from us, nor, of course, from the unprotected Folk or the Humans aboard their flimsy boats. The Folk caught on quickly and seemed to tell the whales what to do, for both species dove deep down beneath our dome-shaped shields, leaving the Humans and their ships to fend for themselves atop the waves. Which is to say, those ships took the shots from the Mengsee starships that managed to blow through or past our shields.

Abruptly, there were Simbara ships in the sky as well, swooping down to fire electrical lightning-bolts from their bushy-branched ships. Where had they come from? I hadn't even seen them arrive.

With two types of attack coming from hundreds of what we must now call *enemy* ships, our shields were not going to hold for long. But we did have some help for the Azureign rebels. It was just not Ayi help.

At first, I saw both Kiké and Deraff freeze in shock. Then Deraff leaped to his paws, or feet, I suppose.

Without a word, he grasped the handles of Kiké's chair and pushed him forward, toward the controls in our now-unmanned tactical area.

"They're killing them!" Calindey shrieked, hands fluttering.

Deraff seated himself and showed Kiké which controls did what. Deraff had already practiced how to aim and fire our defense drones, which would jump in front of a missile, plasma jet, or lightning strike from the Mengsee and Simbara ships. He deployed a wave of those.

Then he moved on to the next step. "Weapons up," the Kynneth purred.

My lady's cry faded. I glanced at her. Her eyes looked shocky, her face pale. Her hands shook. She was incapable of issuing any command, or so it looked to me.

I looked away from her and toward our two non-Ayi volunteers.

"Fire as needed," I told them, exceeding my authority.

Deraff showed Kiké what to do to aim and fire our own plasma cannons. Then Deraff himself began carefully targeting enemy ships and firing the plasma cannon. When that required cooldown, he sent off missiles at Mengsee and Simbara ships.

Kiké seemed to struggle a moment, then at last sent a line of ion fire at the highest layer of the Mengsee ships, who had conveniently placed themselves in neat, layered rows.

Maybe they thought we would not be able to fight. Maybe they thought we would refuse to bring the battle forward from merely *protecting* the rebels to *actively defending* them. They had thoughtlessly arrayed their ships like the Human game of dominos. As the Human youth fired the ion guns, ship after ship collapsed, some hitting their fellows, some beginning a fall toward the planet.

Meanwhile Deraff shot off missiles while the plasma cannon recharged, picking off ship after ship, hitting the same unit until their shields failed and they either fled or blew.

The Mengsee were more than ten ships down before whoever directed their battle took notice of *Star Glow* and our devastating ion gun, plasma cannons and missiles.

Then they turned on us. It looked like a thousand missiles came our way.

I prayed our generators were strong enough to keep both our shields up, over ourselves and the unprotected flotilla below. Our hulls are not impervious, but they are definitely stronger than wooden boats and glass balls. If we had to, we'd put all our shields over the Azureign rebels.

We could jump into null to remove ourselves from the enemy line of fire...but that would leave the Humans and Folk and whales with no protection at all during the moments we would be gone; it was a last-resort move in this case.

Calindey got control of herself and ordered more defensive drones out, as well as a few offensive ones. These she ordered to fire only on Mengsee ships, or only on Simbara.

It was well she gave those drones specific targets, because with a series of nearby jump-out thumps, we were abruptly joined by *more ship*s.

Friendly ones, this time. Ayi ships. All House Dzarn ships, of course, because other houses would have no interest in this small irrelevant planet. At least not until they turned out to be a source of wealth. I am not always proud of my people. Today, I was proud of my House.

I glanced over my shoulder at Calindey. My lady's copper hair strands seemed electrified, flying around her head with a crackle. Then the silvery gray hairs began to move, and so I realized our shields were overloading.

The *pejiin* screen went down briefly, then we were englobed by the other Dzarni ships, who shared their shields with us, as well as dropping them down over the flotilla, which was now in desperate retreat from the isle and the enemy starships.

Calindey's hair went flat. The moment of *pejiin*-overload faded out, and our grav systems and electricals settled back down to something resembling normal.

At the control panel, Kiké was still firing, though I could see Deraff's energy was fading. He banged the console in frustration, then fell off his chair, exhaustion taking over to prevent him from destroying himself by continuing to call on the adrenalin surge that had pushed him this far.

Like a big cat that had run too far, too fast, for too long, he was spent. He would recover, but it took a little time.

Kiké glanced at him, and then apparently reassured, took over firing missiles as well as sending out the last of our defensive drones and firing the ion gun. He did not touch the plasma gun, which probably needed another cool-down by now anyway.

Fortunately, now we had other Ayi ships also acting both defensively and protectively for the allied flotilla. They even sent some offensive fire, using up their own few trained Ayi or Kynnethi fighters.

Even with their help, I saw a whale's pale belly breach the water, as it floated up, upside down, cold in death on our ship's infrared scanner.

Outside our shields.

Surely the Mengsee ships could see this too.

Apparently we were not covering all of the whales, and we had no way to tell them to stay under our shielding dome.

I saw missile after Mengsee missile burst against those combined shields. At the same time, Simbara electrics flashed again and again, lightning-bright against the dark water.

I know I was still numb, but I could not imagine what the two Compact members were thinking.

Why would they do this? Why build the installation at the Preserve at all?

And then why try to hide their actions by destroying—or trying to destroy—these rebels of Azureign?

There were far too many witnesses to their perfidy by now. They should have given up and retreated. But like wild animals in a panic to survive, they kept trying to destroy both the flotilla and its protectors.

—Dzarn Reith Koras, of
Calindey's *Star Glow*

Chapter Ten: The War Expands

Things were bad enough with the addition of the volcano. At least its actions were natural, though the ignition and explosion had been triggered by our sonic attack, the result was something we understood. At least a volcano is explicable.

The next reaction was not.

Blocky stone rectangles raced across our skies and came to a stop above us, with an enormous sonic boom. These ships, with spiky extrusions over them making them look like building-block porcupines, then proceeded to open fire on us. No warning. No ultimatum, just literal fire from starships onto primitive ocean ships.

I could see the *Star Glow* attempting to protect us, as the blocky ships fired down upon the flotilla. Missiles rained down. Streaks of plasma fire that did *not* come from any volcano.

We had never expected the Compact ships to attack us. We had nothing to fight back with. Only the Ayi shields protected us from the projectiles and sun-fire. I thought the ships were Mengsee, by Reith's descriptions I had read. But they did not communicate with us, they just attacked.

Were their buildings at the Preserve worth so much?

We could do little to help ourselves. Certainly our cannons weren't going to reach those ships in our skies, even if we had more ammunition for them. I had seen many crew dumping their cannons overboard, even as they turned their ships and tried to flee. They might have made it, but we lacked the Dolphinfolk help. They'd dived deep when the plasma bolts began raining down.

I cannot fault the Folk for abandoning us, those that had been trying to push all our vessels to safety under the protective shield. The Dolphinfolk were completely unprotected, and those fiery bolts had to hurt, maybe even kill them, if nothing else by boiling the ocean water they hit, even if they missed a direct hit on an individual.

Then another series of sonic booms announced the arrival of bushy Simbaran ships. I was fairly certain these were Simbaran; Reith's descriptions had been given awhile ago, along with descriptions of other species' ships. I might have been confused, but then it didn't make much sense for anyone *else* to be here, attacking us. Not that I can say Mengsee or Simbara had sufficient reason to bring *starships* against us. Not when they *knew* all too well, how primitive our technology is.

The branchy Simbara ships dropped down almost to ocean level and began firing lightning bolts onto and among our boats. Beneath the Ayi shield.

Some of the Mengsee did likewise, coming in slowly to break through the shield, leaving them overly close to us.

So the Folk raced deep under water below the Ayi shields, leaving us on our boats to try and find some kind of safety while the Simbara seemed determined to destroy as many of us as possible.

Three forms of attack landed among us: missiles detonated, blowing entire boats apart into shards of kindling; plasma bolts hit ships, whales and Dolphinfolk alike, turning them into the fires of hell; and third, any rescue of anyone was complicated by lightning bolts zapping everywhere on the water and on the ships.

I don't know what they loaded their cannon with, but I saw one ship's cannoneers fire off *something* which successfully hit a Simbaran ship, knocking off a pair of the long branchy protrusions. That ship immediately fled. The cannoneers had a moment to cheer before a Mengsee plasma gun turned their little ship into a pyre of death.

I saw people swimming in toward the edge of the Ayi shield, trying to get beneath it to save themselves, not realizing it was no longer safe there. The swimmers actually were getting to the shield faster than our boats could, with our weak little solar engines and no Dolphinfolk help. Simbaran ships hit them with lightning, over and over, as if they could somehow make those people more dead.

It made me furious. These aliens knew well how little capability we had: *they'd been the ones that forced these limitations upon us.* And yet they chose to retaliate with *starships* and weapons so advanced they did not even make sense to us.

The only thing that saved any of us was the arrival of more and more Ayi ships, who expanded the shield and strengthened it. A few of them even dropped down to fire weapons upon those enemy ships which had dared go under the dome which was supposed to protect us.

This surprised me because I knew the cost to Ayi of fighting back. That my brother was one of the ones firing, I found out later.

Thus we learned of what the Ayi wanted from us: fighters who could wield weapons and accept fatalities of their targets without harming themselves.

More and more shields dropped over us from the many teardrop-ships that now hovered above us. Rather like the eggs protecting the birds, in a reversal of normality.

The shield protected us also from some of the sounds, some of the volcanic ash and debris from explosions.

But we still could hear a series of thumps as more Ayi ships jumped in.

They were followed by a stream of a third type of ship: black, lumpy coal chunks. I thought I remembered those were Toridani ships.

My heart sank as I saw them, for the Ayi were already outnumbered two to one.

Nearby, another great spear of what seemed to be light stabbed down outside the Ayi shield, to make a pair of our straggling ocean ships just...vanish. And all of their people along with them.

Immediately afterwards, another swirly-bubble dome enveloped us—all of us again, ships, whales, Folk, and gymbals, but not the Preserve or its buildings. There was this one immense bubble, and inside it a bunch of smaller bubbles, or domes, adding as much protection as they could.

I saw one of the lightning spears from a bushy coral-looking Simbara ship hit the Ayi shield-bubble and reflect off at an angle that came close to hitting one of the spiky rectangular Mengsee ships. That seemed fitting, that they might accidentally destroy one another.

"They're out of control!" Gabriel Zev yelled in my ear.

I shook my head. "I cannot understand why they would do all this? Did we hurt them so badly?"

Zev opened his hands, palm up, meaning *I have no idea.* "We have scared them somehow, I think," he said. "They're afraid of us."

Far above us, on the Mengsee side of the confrontation, there was considerable movement as more Ayi ships arrived. The Mengsee clumped up in the sky northwest of us, making chaos of their neat formations.

Apparently, that made them even easier to hit, for the few Ayi ships that were firing weapons managed to blow a whole group apart with what looked like a single missile. The Mengsee ships moved again, scattering into a ragged, disorganized mess. Their rate of firing missiles and plasma bolts onto us was now much reduced.

We now learned the Toridani ships were not here to attack us, but rather to help defend against the other two Compact members that *were* attacking.

There weren't many of the lumps of coal Toridani ships, but they were deadly with their firing patterns, taking out ship after Simbaran ship, without damaging any of our poor people or ships that still struggled to achieve safety inside the Ayi shield dome.

One more set of our cannoneers tried firing their cannon against the few low-flying Simbaran ships that remained, but whatever they'd loaded into their cannon made it explode. And another ship of our little Azureign fleet went to the bottom. After that, no one tried to fight back. We just huddled beneath the dome, or struggled to get there, hoping the Mengsee and Simbara would not notice us.

Last to enter the battle, a fifth group of ships thumped into being in the sky beneath our rings, adding their metallic ovoids to the black Ayi drops and the black coal lumps of our allies.

I had to hope they were allies.

It looked to me like they had *jumped* in, as the Ayi ships did. But I thought Reith had told us *no one* else had random jump drives.

If I went by the shape and color, I would guess these ships belonged to Humanity. Maybe. But I had never seen any starships before we saw that first little black teardrop shuttle of Calindey's. I was guessing, trying to remember Reith's almost off-hand comments and written notes about starships.

What were Humans doing here?

With random jump drives like the Ayi?

Had the Ayi finally given someone else that special drive, or was this something new?

These were questions I could not answer, until later, when we met with representatives of all these people. Honestly, during that part of the battle, there wasn't much we could do but think and guess and watch. We certainly had nothing we could fight back with.

For now, on "our" side of the battle, to the east of the Preserve, the ovoid metallic ships that I thought were Humanity's, adjusted themselves so that each ship of the Mengsee and Simbara was faced one by one, by either an Ayi, Toridani or unknown, possibly Human, ship. *Our* ships.

Could I call them that, "ours?" though we had not been connected to Earth in any way for a millennium?

None of the ships appeared to be firing or otherwise attacking, at first; certainly there were no more spears of plasma or missiles loosed. There were lots of swirly-bubble shields around the various ships, though.

It was a standoff.

With our Ayi advisor gone, we were definitely in over our heads; we had no idea what to do or what was happening.

Nothing we could do was going to affect any of these sky-ships that was certain. If we tried to flee, we'd emerge from beneath the Ayi's protective shield and become vulnerable. We could only stay put and watch.

Altogether, I would estimate, there were 500 alien ships in the sky above us and the Preserve, or what was left of it. The once-neatly arranged Mengsee side was now a chaotically disorganized clump. The Ayi weren't lined up, either. The Toridani were scattered among the unknown-probably-Human ships. One side had two kinds of ships. The other, three. Each ship was matched, one on one.

No one was doing anything visible.

I imagined the people on those ships were talking to each other, trying to avoid more death and destruction. But that apparently did not work.

On the Azure Ocean, beside the still-fuming and lava-drooling volcano, we had a front row seat to the first starship battle anyone from Azureign had ever seen. Or maybe it was a skyship battle, for they were in our atmosphere.

I know that some, perhaps many of our people couldn't even imagine what they were looking at. They had not been prepared with information about aliens, and their ships, and how we were not connected with the rest of Humanity, and most of us did not even know so many aliens even *existed*.

While this had not been planned, had not been expected, at least a few of us had known that such a thing was potentially possible, though we had no explanation for why. I could not imagine what was—or had been—so important on the Preserve that the aliens involved would send *starships* to protect it.

Or maybe, to protect the secret, that the Preserve had ever existed?

A secret now blown wide open, if Toridani, Ayi and Humanity now saw what was going on, which of course, they did.

But the Mengsee and Simbara still did not give up.

We were told later that the Mengsee and Simbara indeed had been running an experiment on Azureign. This they used as their defense when they were hauled before a tribunal of others in the Compact. But more on that later.

The Toridani had been suspicious there was something prohibited going on, and they'd never approved anything about what the Mengsee and Simbara were doing. But their reaction was to wait and watch, not even telling Cuy what they suspected, much less the rest of the Compact.

The Ayi had guessed what might be happening, and had tried to warn others in the Compact, and not one singe species believed that warning. The rest of the Compact could not believe such a thing would happen at all, much less on an interdicted planet, *much less* initiated by aliens of the Compact.

So the Ayi had warned the Humans of Earth, and there they had been believed, but what should Earth do about it?

Now what saved us—at least some of us—was that the friendly Ayi had kept an eye on the two species that ran this experiment, to try to learn what they were up to. That they suspected it was not to Azureign's benefit, and was definitely not to the advantage of the Dolphinfolk, who more and more of them had come to believe are an intelligent species in their own right.

Nothing the Mengsee and Simbara were doing on Azureign was approved by the Compact. Hence their haste to try and cover it up by destroying us and our protest. They now tried to hide the remains of the Preserve itself.

We were astonished to see some missiles shoot down from the boxy Mengsee ships in the sky onto the remaining buildings and ruins of the Preserve, even going so far as to fire onto some remnant works that were in the process of being covered with lava flow from the volcano. Just in case the lava didn't quite do the job, I suppose.

When they were done obliterating the remains of the Preserve, the Mengsee and Simbara turned and fired on Toridani and Human and Ayi ships.

Which fought back. All of them.

The ovoid Human ships had missiles and plasma guns, like the Mengsee. They exchanged near-equal blows with one another.

The Toridani fired on both Mengsee and Simbara. Their primary weapon was similar to the Ayi ion gun: a coherent beam of light or ions that hit with devastating effect, once a ship's shields went down. The limit on these ion beams was their cooldown period. After several minutes of sustained fire to bring down a shield and damage a ship, the beams must shut down. It was kind of like blowing out a very, very hot candle. Then they had to repower/relight it.

During the beam cooldown, the Ayi and Toridani ships fired missiles and scattered drones, like a firetruck spraying water. The drones helped defensively, and I learned later also could show details of the battle. Their cameras could report back things like damage done, real-time-exact ship placement locations and data feedback on enemy ships' shield strength and energy system robustness.

Ayi ion beam fire and missiles went out from a few of their ships, but less than before. They were running out of allies aboard their ships who could do the job. The job of firing weapons, to injure, destroy, kill others.

The job Ayi can barely do for themselves.

I learned later that Kiké continued firing defense drones like a fiend, and Deraff was back in action after a short rest, carefully aiming and firing: one missile, one ship death, repeat.

Whoever was in charge of the other Ayi ships sent an order to *Star Glow,* to jump to null and rest while the rest maintained the shield over us and did what they could to attack enemy ships.

A few Toridani cleaned up the attackers among us, mostly Simbara that had flown low and hit us with their lightning bolts. Now those bushy, coral-spiky ship remnants intermingled with the remains of our flotilla, beneath the shield dome, floating or sinking beneath the waves. We'd become a junkyard of broken ships.

Mengsee and a few Simbara continued to chase some of us, even as our wooden boats and glass gymbals attempted to flee back toward the mainland with the help of a few brave Folk. Ayi ships accompanied those who fled, keeping a shield over them. But most of us had no Dolphinfolk help; our scattered ships bobbed among the remnants of starships on Azureign's Azure Ocean.

I felt like I could *feel* the Mengsee's anger on us, as if I too had *pejiin: How could these colonists, these* children *in the technical sense, dare to attack them!* I imagined they thought this, though of course I could not know.

The Simbara were desultory, as I'd been told was usual, firing upon a ship of the flotilla if it was conveniently right under them, but otherwise, mostly dodging attack, or watching as the Mengsee fiercely attempted to obliterate all the whales, Dolphinfolk or boats in sight.

The Mengsee had lost control of themselves.

I cannot say how Mengsee may ordinarily fight, but it does not seem to me they would usually be so enraged that they were oblivious to their losses, as they were here. They'd have gone extinct by now if that was their normal habit.

154

They were so fierce, not giving an inch. I was afraid our allies might have to destroy every last one of their ships to get this horrendous fight to stop.

But something else happened, instead.

Bursting into the sky beneath our Azureign's pretty rings, came an appalling flash of blazing blue light, and a *huge*, thunderous voice that shook us all to stillness.

"*WHAT IS THIS?*" the voice roared, shaking ground, ocean and air alike.

Amorphous light swirled above the fleets, cohering slowly into vaguely Humanoid, gigantic shapes.

The Cuy had arrived. And they were *angry*.

Chapter Eleven: What We Learned

Before anyone was allowed to leave the Preserve area, we were required to bear witness to the Cuy of all that had been and was still happening upon Azureign: our unrest, the unreasonable actions and non-actions of Mengsee and Simbara. Their manipulation of the Red and our pirates; our Eze's assassination. Our revolt.

The first actual questions was: Why did the Dolphinfolk revolt, and why and how did we join them.

While the Cuy could hear everyone (and possibly read everyone's thoughts), *we could not hear each other,* scattered across an ocean of seawater and sky and ships, as we were.

So the biggest Ayi ship, (which was not *Star Glow,* I noticed) called *Winds of Change* was selected to house and host the various species for a series of meetings. We were to give "Explanations," as the Cuy demanded. Individuals were chosen from among us all to go to that ship.

The meetings, some of which included only two or three individuals along with the Cuy *presences,* were called *Hearings.* The Cuy called forth representatives of all the species involved in each detailed event they wanted clarified.

This included the Dolphinfolk, of course. Rather than take us all down to the ocean again, the Cuy just scooped up a ball of water with three members of the Stormflyer pod, including Whiyira, Singaree and a female whose name I did not know in it. They swam in the enormous bubble of ocean water which was moved swiftly inside the ship, making everyone jump back, although Cuy controlled the bubble's shape so no one who needed to breathe air would be engulfed.

They weren't kept aboard long, but the Cuy "spoke" with them while maintaining the enormous globe of water and air that the three Folk individuals could swim around in.

While no humans participated, we were allowed to observe.

In the water along with some seaweed and fish, I saw a single Human artifact swirl about. Obvious even in that enormous bubble of ocean water was some person's toggle button that had come off their shirt. Being made of tree bark, it had a tendency to float, but pressure from the Folk's fins churning the water as they moved about pushed it down and around. My eyes followed it as it spun around, a tiny bit of Humanity's trash that had been caught up in this important moment.

It didn't matter that the person who had worn the shirt hadn't intended that to happen. They'd probably have been happy to have the toggle back. They hadn't ripped it from their shirt and thrown it into the water on purpose. But. It was these sorts of random unintended effects that were as important as our intended ones in our interactions with the sea and everything in it on Azureign.

At that moment, I think I came to understand why the Dolphinfolk asked for their own planet. One with no other people on it of any kind, just fish and whales and the various normal creatures of the sea, the domain of the Folk, and no one else.

We were the cause of junk in their water, as well as the damage to their social system caused by taking whole pods to Help us. They hoped to be free of that. It was as important to them as getting away from all Dirt People or Sky People "rules" or control.

I did not blame them. It did make me sad, though, that even on our low-tech interdicted planet, we Humans couldn't seem to control our mess.

Cuy did not respond to any of our requests or questions, saying a judgement would come when all had been heard.

Meanwhile, we were to remain aboard *Winds of Change.*

And here I met my first Human from Earth. As you might expect, but I had been uncertain of, we looked alike.

The Earth Humans were on average somewhat bigger and older than the Azureign representatives. But like us, their skin and hair came in all different colors and textures and styles, and they were different shapes and sizes, and all of us more or less spoke Common and wore roughly similar clothes.

Representing the Humans of Azureign were myself of Tehassa, Tae the Pirate Queen of Jia, and Gabriel Zev of Maladh.

I'd borrowed a clean white linen shirt, but still wore the second pair of linen pants I'd brought for the sea journey and battle, which were now no longer clean. The Ayi helped us out with showers or baths, and some system that quickly cleaned our clothes and returned them.

Both Zev and I were barefoot, though I saw Queen Tae had managed to bring or acquire a pair of delicate embroidered slippers, and a much more elegant outfit than we two males had. My thought was we hadn't planned on anything fancy for celebrating the end of our fight, but there was Tae, refuting our argument and looking quite lovely.

I noticed her grin as she looked at Gabriel Zev with sparkling eyes. At the same time she more or less ignored me, and I ended up feeling relief; she didn't seem to care for me much more than I did her, so that wasn't a thing that I needed to worry about. In fact, I hadn't thought about my future at all for many days, and marriage dropped to last in the list of future concerns.

I decided that what I would do would depend upon how these meetings turned out. I still had my phone, which I had been told would still work. I used it to call the Zeen, to let her know I was safe, and what we were doing. She began yelling at me to send Kiké back and would not listen to anything I had to say, so I ended the call.

I then called Zola and spent awhile describing what had happened to end the starship fight, which she had not seen. She seemed far more interested than my mother had been. After that peaceful interaction, she also yelled at me for "letting" Kiké join *Star Glow* for the battle, so I hung up on her, too. She called back and I did not respond. I was not going to accept being blamed for what was beyond my control.

The fact was, Kiké had been safer than I had been, by far. And he had enjoyed himself, and had felt competent and helpful and proud. I had no intentions of letting anyone ruin that.

I wish I had greater powers of description, to tell you what the spaceship looked like inside.

Like *Star Glow, Winds of Change* had a waterfall and fountain in a park. There was also a stream that ran from the base of the waterfall and wound around several large open social areas, or parklike arenas of the ship.

Early one morning, I received notice I must attend one of the hearings. I'd already had an excellent breakfast, complete with good coffee (or some kind of substitute that was indistinguishable from the real thing: so Ayi know about Humans and their coffee!)

It turned out that this hearing was with Mengsee and Simbara. The Cuy ran the meeting, their glistening forms morphing through various shapes and colors which might have explained some of what they thought and felt, but which also could just as well have meant nothing. They were interesting to watch. I much preferred staring at the Cuy than at the insectoid Mengsee representatives, and the slug or caterpillar-like green Simbara.

The Cuy asked why they had interfered with the interdicted planet, Azureign.

There was no response that made sense to me for awhile, as the aliens communicated (or really, failed to communicate) with anyone beyond the Cuy, for they ignored us altogether. Finally some sort of signal was given, and a translator stepped forward to describe what was being "said" or transmitted via other means than sound.

The Mengsee said they were trying to find out what Humans would do when we were boxed into a corner. They said they wanted to see how acquisitive Humanity would be if both they and the Mengsee or they and the Simbara ended up wanting the same stellar and planetary real estate.

Would Humans just seize the land from others? Would they try to bargain?

No one really came out and said that their "experiment" on Azureign was *human vs. human.* They'd set it up with the Red (humans) attacking Jia and Maladh (humans). How was that a test of what we would do against Mengsee or Simbara?

And also, no one mentioned that assassinating the Eze of Tehassa wasn't going to tell them what Humans would do versus any alien species at any particular star system we both wanted. Anger at these contradictory "explanations" simmered in my heart.

Like human lawyers, the Mengsee were trying to argue their way out of being held responsible for their people's actions.

But I gathered that somehow, the Cuy realized these inconsistencies, or had understood them before the Mengsee even tried to explain.

The "lead" Cuy—the one who asked the most questions—turned to us three Humans and asked (I think inside my head, because I thought it more than heard it) if what we had done in Jia and Maladh and Tehassa was the same as what we would do if we claimed the same real estate as another star-spanning species.

This was difficult to answer, because for all of us, our homes on Azureign were a different and more meaningful thing than a hypothetical new colony on a far-flung planet might be. I mean, we don't even have decent sailing ships, much less starships, much less an opportunity to sail(?) among the stars and settle on new colony worlds...

I received a sense of amusement from the Cuy mind or minds that were communicating with us.

"Wouldn't it be better to ask Humans from Earth that question?" Tae asked aloud.

"We on Azureign only recently learned so many other species even exist, so it is a far bigger step for us to imagine establishing a colony, than it would be for Humans on a starship," I said, trying to support what the Queen of Pirates had said.

Would you have fought back, here on Azureign, if you could?

I think all three of us were immediate and the same in our response. *Yes.*

"We wanted to defend our homes," I said, and beside me Gabriel Zev nodded his head.

My mind wanted to wander off, wondering if Cuy understood human body language, but the Cuy asked:

Would you wish things were the way they used to be?

161

Here our three answers were slower and much less aligned.

I said, "I would certainly wish my father was still alive."

Tae said, "My people of Jia are suffering."

Zev had an angry expression on his face, but his words were calm enough: "Revenge is mine, sayeth the Lord." He swallowed and raised his head to stare back at what passed for the Cuy's face. "Because we are not well-suited to decide how to exact revenge. But I would like to go kick the Red out of Lyang City, and let my family take control of the government again. I think we need to make some changes, but far less radical ones than the Red are trying to make."

"People are starving," Tae said.

"People are confused," I added.

Are you angry at Mengsee and Simbara?

This time we three were more in agreement. "More like extremely confused and frustrated."

If you had the capability to blow up the Oracle like you did the Preserve, would you do so?

"The Oracle has not been helpful."

"We need modern help, with technology, medicine, agriculture..."

"I want to go home," Zev finished. No one said yes.

Do you think the Dolphinfolk should be free? Do they deserve their own planet?

Yes, we all said.

"Though I hope it doesn't have to be Azureign, because where would *we* go?" I added.

I felt a sense of warmth cover me, as the Cuy seemed to think about things while offering assurance we were heard.

Return in three days, the Cuy told us.

There was time between sessions that I was expected to attend that was awkward to fill. I could sleep, or eat. I had no books I could read, but I did look at the pictures in a few Human-type book cubes that had been left in the sleeping quarters on *Winds of Change* that I shared with Gabriel Zev.

A couple young, giggling Ayi girls showed up at our door and invited Zev and I on a tour of their *kej*. I wanted to see more of the ship, so I gladly accepted, as did Zev. It would have been difficult to turn them down, I think, they were so excited and proud to show us their home.

We toured what I would call the "bridge" first, and saw a pair of Kynnethi youths sitting at the tactical area (as Kiké later explained). We had no language in common but they smiled and waved their tails at us, which made the Ayi girls giggle again.

Next they took us to and around another, bigger park than the one I'd previously seen. It also had a waterfall, a stream, and plantings of trees and flowers sufficiently different from anything I'd seen before that I was immediately enchanted. It was beautiful and peaceful.

Then we were led to (one of the) kitchens—galley, I suppose—and shown the food preparation area, and the dining room where dozens of people of various ages and races were eating. So far Gabriel and I had eaten in our room, from food we had ordered and that had been brought to us. We hadn't known a more public place was even available.

"I'm going to want to come back here and have some of that chicken, or whatever it is," Gabriel said, and I laughed.

I think the girls understood him, as they laughed too. Then one of them tried to tell us something, I'm guessing their name for the fowl we'd identified as chicken, but we all ended up confused and laughing.

They took us to the entrance of the "private" areas of the ship, or city, I suppose. Here they were able to explain, "No," meaning neither of us Humans (males?) were allowed to go in. This explanation was reinforced by two serious-looking young men (I am guessing about the sexes, here, though I think Ayi are similar enough to Humans that I was not wrong). These guards stepped across the entrance and looked very sternly at us.

"No," one of the girls said again.

"Okay!" Gabriel said, and nodded. We walked away from that area and down a fairly long corridor.

I tried not to feel like a dog being trained.

"Guest rooms," one of our guides said, waving a hand at the many doors that lined the hall. She had trouble pronouncing the hard "g," tending to swallow it and sort of cough.

"Observation!" the other one said as we stepped into a room that had one colossal curved wall that was...well, a window, I suppose. A window, or gigantic viewport into space.

It caught at me, that view.

I stood and stared at thousands and thousands— millions—of stars. I suppose some of them were distant galaxies that were so far from us they were just a single point of light. Others were more obvious as swirls of a spiral galaxy among the individual stellar systems.

The stars were so beautiful. They were, to me at that time, beacons of hope and opportunity. From such a distance we could not see any planets they might have, nor any people those planets might bear, squabbling, loving, making messes and cleaning them up. We saw only the purity of starlight.

I could feel tears well up in my eyes as I stared at them, points of light in an infinite blackness.

It did not occur to me to be embarrassed about my tears until the girls suggested it was time to leave.

They spoke in soft tones, and gently brushed my arm to get my attention.

When I turned to them, I saw that Gabriel Zev was gone. Only myself and the two Ayi girls populated that wondrous room. I could not understand why *everyone* was not there.

My two guides did not giggle as they quietly led me back to my room and the areas of the *kej* I was familiar with.

I turned to them, outside my door. "Thank you," I said. And they smiled gentle Mona Lisa smiles at me before they turned away to go on about their business.

Those stars had an enormous and lasting impact on me. I cannot explain why, but suddenly to me, all the petty details of Azureign and its people no longer mattered.

A fire had been lit within me.

A fire to travel to those stars.

INTERVAL: The Human Weakness

Here is the thing about Humanity that I think caused the Mengsee to panic.

Humans *survive*.

Whatever horrible or splendid circumstances they are dropped into, they attempt to make do. Masters of improvisation, they fight when necessary, and they are willing to work hard. They puzzle things out, think things through...in order to survive, which they are indeed good at. It seems to be a result of their particular combination of curiosity and innate strength.

Yes, they are also proud, arrogant, independent (perhaps too much so), and they *hate* letting others have control over them; they want, even need, to be self-governed. They are strong.

For these reasons, they tend to scare (other) peoples, as they did Mengsee.

These traits of Humans are definitely the species' weakness in the minds of Cuy. But Cuy cannot blame the Humans for the Mengsee actions, no matter how much they might have frightened them.

Certainly some of the difficulties between Humans and Mengsee revolve around Azureign being an interdicted planet for far, far too long.

Which almost excuses Mengsee. Almost.

Sometimes I am afraid of Humans, too. When Zeden Kell stands before me, seeming so confident, so secure in himself, so alive. When Kiké grabs the controls of my *kej*-ship and manages to defend us, so easily.

But then I sense them in *pejiin*, and I see something else. I see Kiké's uncertainty in himself. I see Zeden's belief that he is perhaps a fool—that I would never have found out if I had just *looked* at him, at his people, as Mengsee have done for a thousand years.

Learning from my friend who lives in *Winds of Change* of Zeden's tears, that came when he stood and looked at the stars, explains everything about Humanity that we believe is good.

Their sense of wonder and awe at the universe that we all too easily forget. In that way, they and the Kynneth are both our teachers.

Yes, some species will wonder if either Mengsee or Humanity is a trustworthy ally, though in my personal opinion, Humans handled themselves throughout these events far better than Mengsee did. Or than don't-ever-be-caught-leading-*anything* Simbara did.

So I believe Humanity's position among Compact members has changed for the better, even though they have yet to make upward progress through the Matrix of Ascension. And Cuy do approve of and even like Humans.

Of course, as full members of the (old) Compact, Humanity as a whole could pretty much do what they wanted before now, as long as they didn't attack other members.

Now, even though Mengsee are wary, we Ayi have taken many more Humans onto our *kej*-ships. Cuy have accepted that this is a thing that needs to happen to help us defend ourselves, especially now that they have seen the flaw in the Kynneth, that they cannot maintain even a defensive much less offensive posture for any length of time.

Small changes move us all forward.

Cuy have decided. The old Compact will be dissolved. It did not work as well as they would have liked.

It permitted this adversity upon Azureign. And other evils.

A new confederation, as yet unnamed, will be formed in its place. This new group, probably to be called the Array, if Cuy have their way—and they will—takes into consideration what the various species *want*, as well as what they are like, at this time.

So, we Ayi want Human help to defend ourselves.

The Mengsee are afraid of competition, and want reassurance that their needs will be met, and that they can keep their distance from Humanity in the future.

Simbara (weirdly to me given their recent behavior) want for all species to be friends. A little impossible, but nice, I guess. They hoped Mengsee and Humans would somehow sort out Azureign and become friendly with one another. Naive, passive, Simbara were somewhat taken in by the Mengsee, in most peoples' opinion. Cuy aren't even angry at them.

The Toridani want very much to not fight Humanity, and would prefer that all their future territories are far away from those claimed by Humans. Here I wonder if they are not a little like Mengsee, perhaps a bit afraid of this flexible, adaptable species.

Cuy, as always, want to teach and to know.

Who else? Yes:

The Dolphinfolk want to be free from human restraint.

This they achieved, for the Cuy found them a planet they will be taken to. They may choose to stay on Azureign or be moved to their own new home, where humans will not be permitted to live. Their fellow ocean inhabitants will be split as well, some to go to the new Dolphinfolk home, some to remain. And on Azureign, Dolphinfolk Help will no longer be needed, since Humans have been freed of the limitations the Compact interdiction had imposed.

This means they will build ships with engines strong enough to sail Azureign's oceans. It means also they will build sky-ships to carry cargo around their planet. Technology will be limited, but not to the extent it once was. They have been given the lesson of Earth, and the long reparations Humanity had to make to restore their home planet to its original natural beauty and balance, once they realized how much damage had been done by centuries of careless "advances."

So the Dolphinfolk have been informed, and they have been given these two options: stay and live with Humans on Azureign...but they will not be forced to Help or contact Humanity, unless they choose to...or they may go to their own planet.

They are considered an intelligent species in their own right, now, and have been given a place in the Matrix of Ascension. Humanity was chosen to mentor them here on Azureign, with more Cuy help than usual, if needed.

For example, they may someday wish to travel among the stars, which will require special starships to accommodate them. This may require some help from Binsanta or the aquatic race of Mengsee, which I suppose Cuy would need to mediate, as well as their Human mentors' help to build such ships.

At the moment, however, the Dolphinfolk do not seem interested in going into space. A few have inquired about their forebears on Earth, but even those did not seem eager to go visit them.

At this time, about half the Folk desire transport to Glia! (meaning water), their new home. The remainder wish to stay on Azureign—mostly those who were already in the habit of speaking to Humans. They and their ocean friends have made the remnants of the Preserve their capital, their home and breeding ground on Azureign. Humans are asked to stay away.

Glia! is yet to be explored, but from the descriptions, it is a glorious water world that should appeal to them—as I would expect from Cuy who found it for them.

Last in this summary, but not at all least, Azureign has been freed of the interdiction and all limits on development.

Humans from Earth have taken an interest in the colonists' plight, and are perhaps even a little angry at how long and under what conditions the colonists have been required to exist. They hope to amend those conditions as soon as possible.

I was glad to see that Tingh Tae Lha, Queen of Pirates, will remain in Jiaru, while her brother, the rightful heir to Jia's crown for the remainder of Tingh's turn in the Rota, will take over in Lyang City as Jia is restored to their previous government system. Hopefully he can clean up the mess the Red have made of things there.

Gabriel Zev has asked Tae to marry him, but is uncertain how that will be resolved, since he needs to return to Maladh to help his own people back to some sort of normalcy, while Tae will stay in Jiaru. Perhaps Zev will abdicate and Maladh will develop a new government, I cannot predict.

Zeden has his own story to finish, and I step aside and give him room to do that, for he is now my brother, so far as two young males from two different species can be such.

Cuy are at peace, my Lady Calindey is respected for her stance in protecting the Azureign colonists, and I am happy at her side.

—Dzarn Reith Koras, of
        Calindey's *Star Glow*

Chapter Twelve: Effects of a Minor War

At the next meeting with Cuy, it was just us and them, no Mengsee and no Simbara.

And at that meeting, we at last received some explanations.

Why Mengsee, in particular had dared to run an experiment on an interdicted planet. Why they—and the Simbara to a lesser degree—had wanted to study Humanity, and had manipulated the governments of several of our nations, to see what we might do.

The Mengsee are afraid, Cuy told us.

Afraid of *us.* Humans in general, and especially what we of Azureign might do once freed from the interdiction.

They thought we would take over the galaxy, I guess. But in a way, that really made no sense. Humans on Earth and our several other colonies had not done so. Why should we of Azureign be seen as potentially different? This has yet to be answered to my satisfaction.

The Cuy reassured us several times that what was done on Azureign was a completely wrong action on Mengsee's part, and was now over with.

The Mengsee, and to a lesser degree Simbara, are to make reparations on Azureign, and then depart the planet, never to return. Cuy said.

Cuy had already set out and told them what exact reparations to make and how they are to be done. We were informed that their atonement had already begun in terms of removing the Red from Jia and Maladh and returning those various people to their original homes.

Tae raised an eyebrow at this, but Zev seemed satisfied.

For Tehassa, of course, they cannot bring your father back to life. However the meddling the Mengsee have done among Corrigan and the pirates is being undone.

Financial remunerations are being given to all three of your nations.

What you individuals choose to do is now entirely up to you, but you will have the aid of Humans from Earth so much as you want it.

Your medical systems will be improved first. Food production and technical help for sailing your oceans will begin next.

The Oracle will be taken over by Humanity with the help of Ayi, so that things move forward as quickly as they can without destroying your world's economies.

I guess what the Cuy decided (without our input on the details) was all right. Honestly, I felt my interest in Tehassa wane as the stars lured me more and more.

Eventually, we who were left returned to our homes. That is to say, most of us did.

Kiké is staying with his friend Derraff on board *Sky Glow*. The Ayi are giving him help to overcome the defect that prevented his legs from developing properly. He is seen as a valued member of the *Sky Glow kej*, and is proud of that.

I learned the lesson that my brother had to teach me: Here on *Winds of Change*, I was not clumsy, nor awkward nor superfluous. Rather than trying to be something I am not, I simply needed to find my right place.

Here with the Ayi we are both needed and could contribute something they required that they did not already have. And they *like* us.

I know Mother will not understand. I simply told her it was part of the settlement. That Kiké was happy and as healthy as he could be. That he has friends. And that he is not coming back.

I journeyed to Montmarras to tell her this, and to explain what I could of the Mengsee and what they had done to us on Azureign. I knew she would not ever see it as I had, who had been on board a tiny wooden boat while starships zoomed overhead firing lethal weapons at one another—and us.

That changed me, too. As much as that vision of the stars had. And so I knew also I could never explain to Mother how I had changed and why I made the decision I did.

I simply informed her of how things were going to be, with her in charge of Tehassa now, as she is, and Zola would follow afterwards.

And that I was abdicating and leaving the planet, probably never to return.

I believe I shocked her.

My sister understands, I think. She hugged me and waved goodbye as I stepped back aboard the *Winds of Change* shuttle. I smiled at the Zeen and the Le'ul of Tehassa, and then I left them behind.

TO THE READER

I try to write a complete novel when I present an Azureign story, but this time I ended up at an awkward point. I could include the Kell's story and Tehassa's role in the actual war (and its aftermath), in the previous book, The Pirate Queen, with Tingh Tae Lha's story. I felt this would have produced an enormous and complex book, which would not focus as closely on either protagonist as I wished to.

Or, I could choose to do what I have done here: tell the stories separately, which means two fairly short novels for the buildup to Azureign's war with the Compact, the war itself, and the aftermath.

I hope you will enjoy them both!

If you would like to correspond with the author or receive infrequent updates about Legends of Azureign, you can send an email to Legends.of.Azureign at gmail.com.

PEOPLE

HUMANS, or DIRT PEOPLE

Note: Tehassa was settled by peoples primarily from Nigeria, Chad, and the region once known as Ethiopia and surroundings, including many tribal minorities, with their own languages.

The compromise official languages for all Tehassans are Swahili and Common, but all tribal groups are encouraged to maintain their own language or dialect as well.

Religious affiliation is by personal choice, though many have settled on Mawu, the female divine creator; originally (it is thought) to have been a Dahomey belief. Vodoun is frowned upon but not actively discouraged.

HUMANS

TEHASSA:

Achojah Lawal—Governor of Isubu Omi (middle island between Montmarras and Mer).

Adaoma Idris—(f) Minister for Transportation

Arvid TenStar—suitor to Zola

Bougainville—high-ranked Tehassan family

Chondu Bello—Tehassan Minister for Education (perpetually late)(m)

Corrigan—enemy of Kell

Dezmon—Zola's childhood friend, not noble

Engde Bassa—Dragonrider based in Mers; her gold and brown dragon is Omanda, Queen and leader of the Mers pack

Eyitayo Musa—(f) Minister for Health & Welfare

Inry Bougainville—suitor to Zola

Jed Fell—Dragonrider based at Mers; his olive green dragon is Odalie

Jereth Corrigan—(like Tengda, also hopelessly in love with Prince Zeden but in his case, Zeden is unaware)

Juwon Yahaya—(m) Minister of Agriculture (including beasts of air, land and sea)

Kezar—Eze (king) of Tehassa Zola, Zeden and Kiké's father; a kind man; a little stupid but not foolish

Kiké—youngest son of Kezar and Zohari; Ras (prince) of Tehassa, second in line to throne after Zeden

K!elli!—usually shortened & simplified to Kell; family name of ruling house in Tehassa (! is a click or tongue cluck sound)

La!ima—family that fully supports Kell (! = a tongue cluck); sometimes spelled Lakima)

Musa Beyn—Mayor of Montmarras

Musa Ibrahim—Minister of the Watch (closest position they have for a War leader)

Nkoma Dabada—Dragonrider based in Mers; his blue-green dragon is Okomo

Nneka Salisu—Minister of the Treasury (n?)

Obi Suleimon—Governor of Mers Island & Mayor of Mers city

Pers Swansson—Dragonrider based in Mers; his golden brown dragon is Oslo

Tengda La!ima—(hopelessly in love with Prince Zeden, who likes but isn't sure he loves her in return)

TenStar—competing ruling house

Zeden Kell—Ras and Le'ul (crown prince) of Tehassa, Zola's younger brother and heir to the throne (male succession)(narrator)

Zohari Kell—Zeen (consort of the Eze, queen) of Tehassa, Zeden, Kiké and Zola's mother

Zola Kell—Ras (princess) of Tehassa (extremely smart, gifted in diplomacy, languages)

OTHERS (not from Tehassa):

Alexa Del Rosario—mayor of Xi, known as the Lady of Xi

Byeol—the Ranger chosen to represent Rangers in Jiaru's council meetings; bears a heavy red beard and mustache; visits Tehassa

Gabriel Reza Zev-—ex-prince of Maladh; one of Tae's suitors at Lyang City; now an ally of the Queen of Pirates at Jiaru

Micki Thomas—Dragonrider of Jiaru pack; her dragon is Quorum

Nan Rian Tingh—oldest brother, former Prince of Jia; often called 'Rian by his sister Tae

Suwan Chatri—leader of the Dragonrider pack sent to Jiaru; her dragon is Paqua

Tae Lha Tingh—Queen of Pirates at Jiaru

Tomoko Hatanaka—leader of the pirates who run Jiaru town and formerly preyed on Azure Sea shipping; also formerly a trader

AYI and OTHERS:

Calindey (properly, Dzarn Calindey Ashana)—Ayi female who
        uses her ship to help at Jiaru, and later at Tehassa, the
        Oracle, and the Preserve
Deraff—Kynneth (a.k.a. Casakin) aboard *Star Glow* who
        befriends Kiké
Reith Koras—Ayi observer and liaison in Tehassa from *Star
        Glow* who narrates the Ayi action
Vadi—Ayi youth who accompanies Zola to the Oracle

DRAGONRIDERS:
Engde Bassa—based in Mers; her gold and brown dragon is
        Omanda is Queen and leader of the Mers pack
Lon Diderot—his inky black dragon (f) is Quita; based at
        Jiaru; interfaces with Dragonriders of Mers in Tehassa
Jed Fell—based in Mers, Tehassa; his olive green dragon is
        Odalie (they tease him about his name)
Micki Thomas—her dark green dragon (m) is Quorum
Nkoma Dabada—based in Mers; his blue-green dragon is
        Okomo
Pers Swansson—based in Mers; his golden brown dragon is
        Oslo
Suwan Chatri—lead Dragonrider at Jiaru; her dragon Paqua
        (Queen) is bright yellow & orange ombre

DOLPHINFOLK
(a note on Dolphinfolk pronunciation:
        "s" is whistled
        ! is a typical dolphin click
        * is a beak gnash or chomping sound
        ing is sounded as a swallow or gulp)

*yssa—member of Whreng! pod at Tehassa
Fossas—member of Whreng! pod at Tehassa
Ingda—co-leader of Whreng! pod at Tehassa
Singaree—member of Stormflyer pod, who interfaces between
        Tehassa's Whreng! pod based at Mers and the Folk War
        Leader
SplitFin—member of Whreng! pod at Tehassa
Whiyira—leader of Stormflyer pod, War Leader for all Folk

Dolphinfolk Pods:

Slickwater   once of Lyang City, now at Jiaru
SoLowBeach   home is Jiaru
Stormflyer   lead pod, home is Long-Arc Archipelago
Whreng!   Tehassa pod (Whreng! means swift)

Dolphinfolk meanings

In Speech:

Barkers   seals, and probably also sea lions
chirps   or chitters, how the Folk communicate amongst
               themselves
Dirt People   Human settlers on Azureign
Glia!   water, new home
Sky people   aliens of the Compact, who are heartily disliked.
               (They usually lump Ayi in with the Humans.)
Singers   big cousins, or whales

In Body Language:

Bubble fence used to confuse and trap schools of fish; used
among other Folk to signal a desire for privacy
Tail stand   greeting
Tail dance   laughter, happiness
Fin slap   (in water) (loud) expression of displeasure,
               disagreement
Flipper flap   (in air) shrug, no opinion
Whistle   expression of enthusiasm

ALIENS or SKY PEOPLE/COMPACT SPECIES:

Ayi—Human-like bipeds with empathic abilities; spaceships &
landers look like black pearls
Casakin (also called Kynneth)—bipedal, furred, catlike;
considered not as smart as Humans or Ayi; they use Ayi
ships and help defend them
Cuy—amorphous, most advanced life forms in the known
universe; they don't have bodies, therefore don't have ships
Deesangua—bipeds of various bright colors; ships are
segmented vee-shapes with disconnected drive pods; fairly
new to Compact; very independent
Humanity—includes Humans and some bioengineered
colonists & traders; atmosphere-capable ships tend to be

178

teardrop shaped; space-only ships tend to be globular, with some cargo / factory ships that are clusters of segments

Mengsee—many differently-shaped species; most commonly encountered is the insectoid six-legged type with exoskeleton. Love mechanical devices; ships are rectangular with a pointed nose on landers, broad wings and spikes protrude all over (unknown purpose)

Simbara—green, slightly Humanoid gastropods; unipedal ("slugfoots"); ships look like coral, or bushes (organic, with spiky branches all over; think of a tumbleweed)

Toridani—mysterious; they communicate only with Cuy via electronics; ships look like lumps of coal, or fire-hardened asteroids (black and lumpy)

Xiariu—new; methane-breathers; no other information

NON-COMPACT SPECIES

Ekkatt—Once a Simbara Helper species that created its own colonies and refused to sign Compact; ships are modeled somewhat like Ayi ships

Forerunners—ancient extinct species (or several?) that developed civilization before Cuy became unbound travelers; possibly destroyed themselves

Jacqua—furry bear-like bipeds, former Compact members who were interdicted to their home world and two colonies; after their revolt, they left the Compact. Ships are reddish-gray, and look like spongy-surfaced flatirons

Kimi—navy blue bipedal species; deep blue vee shaped ships; extremely aggressive, esp. toward Ayi

Minka—unknown and unknowable; they avoid areas where Compact exists, but will open fire if they encounter any other ships; powerful weapons, but they do not seek out contact; ships are ovoid or rectangular and glassy-looking

Zenaan—confined to their own solar system (interdicted)

THINGS and CRITTERS

Critters

Freedom Tae's mustang horse, a pinto, traded from Hei Mu

Paqua bright yellow and orange Queen dragon of the Jiaru pack; her rider is Suwan Chatri

Quita Lon Diderot's inky black dragon; one of 3 dragons in Jiaru pack

Quorum Micki Thomas's dark green dragon of the Jiaru pack

Things

anisa algae —a type of edible seaweed-algae that only grows in the Azure Sea of south Jia

bandova—melon like fruit; dragons love it and can quickly destroy a field

barkers—what Dolphinfolk call seals

basket (gondola)—the place where passengers stand

Benqi fruit —used often by travelers, benqi has a tough, thick, skin and actually tastes better when a few days overripe. The melon-like fruit comes from a vine discovered on an early colony world of Earth and is often included in seed banks for new colonies. It is becoming a staple on Azureign, because it is willing to grow anywhere, though some dislike it because it can become a pest in well-watered areas.

biodiesel—low-energy diesel fuel produced from vegetable oils, burned to create the hot air to provide lift for balloons, and used to power some ships in addition to solar-powered motors

bodhaata—ungulates similar to antelope or kangaroo

burner—propels heat into the envelope of a balloon, using a type of biodiesel fuel; cargo balloons usually have several burners to provide enough lift for heavier loads

celluwrap or cellubags—thin wrap or containers made from cellulose (replaces many plastic wrap uses)

Chem-O-Color—or Chem rug—living carpet or fabric that changes color depending upon what it is "fed" and how it is "set"

drag rope—on a balloon, the drag rope is deployed on landing to drag on the ground to slow the balloon; it also gives wranglers a way to tether the balloon

envelope—the "bag" that contains the hot air on a balloon; made from silk, gores are stitched into squared-off triangles, wide at the top (crown) and narrow at the bottom (skirt) where it attaches to the basket. The skirt is coated in thin plass to fireproof it. Seams are likewise plass-coated for strength.

feurla tree—a non-Earth tree with red leaves, scarlet flowers and sweet black edible fruit; the wood resembles mahogany and is used for carvings and small furnishings

fin slap (in water)—Dolphinfolk gesture of anger, disapproval

fin (flipper) flap (in air)—Dolphinfolk shrug; don't know/don't care

glia!—Dolphinfolk for water, ocean

gymbal balls, gymbals—Helper species; a plant that grows huge, sturdy glass-like spheres within spheres, useful as housing in the desert and plains of Azureign

plass, plassceramic—resinous semi-liquid ceramic that is flexible and castable until exposed to air, then it remains flexible for about a day, then dries firm to hard. Made mostly of sand; Compact approved building material used for many things (replacing all concrete and many plastic uses)

platecone—non-Earth tree that grows on Azureign; edible seeds are held in series of plate-like rings on the cone; the wood is useless for anything but firewood, but the trees grow well and wild all across central Azureign

querfufu—kind of a cross between the town drunk and an idiot Uncle; a clumsy inadequate person

rip panel—piece of a balloon's envelope that can be pulled (ripped) free to quickly deflate the envelope

tail-stand—used by Dolphinfolk to rise out of the water to speak, using the tail flukes to remail elevated; a greeting

tail-dance—a sign of Folk amusement, or laughter: a tail stand combined with half-spins, little jumps or bounces up from the water, and head bobs

AZUREIGN COLONY TIMELINE*

Earth Years (C.E.)	Galactic Era (G.E.)	Event
2450		Azureign is discovered by human explorers
2495		Pre-terraform studies are complete
2499		TerraForm Corp. operations begin
2924		Wars of Succession on Earth; contact with all colonies stops
3101		Records destroyed; Azureign lost along with others
3220	1	First contact; Galactic Era begins
	25	Compact signed on Terran colony Oni
	191	Azureign "rediscovered"
	211	Rules of Settlement created as part of Compact; signed on Earth
	242	Economic plan for Azureign finalized
	289	Azureign Oracle installation is complete
	292	Library of Humanity is complete and hidden
	295	First Landing: colonists of the first wave arrived and are abandoned
	388	Compact allows Second Landing on Azureign
	677	Oracle updated; Azureign economic plan updated by Compact without Earth's approval or signature
	1315	(the present)

*discovered in Azureign's Library of Humanity

EARTH COLONIES

NAME	Year founded	Year settled	Population*	Description**	Status
Ahura Mazda	2939	?	0.4	formidable weather	extinct?
Ariel	3100	3191	125		interdicted
Azureign	2450	295 GE	720	storms, wild oceans	unknown
Comarre	3034	3080	1,125	perfect	thriving
Denali ***	444 GE	444 GE	1	moderate	low population
Eshu	2420	414? GE	0.5	missing minerals	unknown, lost?
Nngara	3139	3212	1.5	difficult	low population
Nur	3030	~233 GE	77	moderate	developing
Oni	2620	111 GE	2,250	pleasant	thriving
Raphael	2412?	388 GE	626		Interdicted
Sandovar	2995	?	?	difficult	?
St. Helena	3111	512 GE	880	pleasant	developing, low population
Tìrwãl	502 GE	595 GE	55	water world	low population
Xander	?	~275 GE	898	Moderate	moderate

* population in millions at last recorded census
** overall ecology/difficulty of establishment
*** aka New Home
Note: 3220 of Earth's CE (Common Era) = 1 GE (Galactic Era)

THE COMPACT

1. Exploration is permitted only in each species' assigned sector.

2. Colonization must be pre-approved after detailed ecological studies.

3. No planet may be altered solely in order to make it more livable for any particular species.

4. No compact signatory may attack any other member's colonies or Home world for any reason.

5. Colonies of signatories must abide by the Rules of Settlement, Ecological Balances (specific to each world), and Fair and Balanced Economies where required (as in interdicted colonies, or special case ecologies).

6. Signatories must promptly supply their assessed "sufficient force" of armed ships to aid any other member when called, to resist outside attack or rebellion. (Mutual military support.)

7. Likewise any member may call for assistance if attacked.

8. Free trade among signatories can *only* be accomplished at Trade Centers, under all-Compact-member oversight, with the exception of medical information, equipment or techniques.

9. Medication information, equipment and techniques may be traded outside of Trade Centers, as needed.

10. Each signatory is expected to build and maintain an orbital Trade Center within 12-20 LY of Home planet. Staff must be representative of all Compact species.

11. Complementing each Trade Center, a Hospital must be built and maintained in orbit, with additional units or clinics within nearby stable gravity locales to supplement

treatments, as necessary. Both shall be equipped, supplied and staffed sufficient to treat all Compact species.

12. All research of any weapons systems must be pre-approved by a majority of Compact members.

13. All Trade of any weapons systems must be pre-approved by a plurality of Compact members.

14. Enslavement of any species is prohibited on all signatory colonies. Home worlds are exempt; except that trade may be limited with Compact members, if slavery does exist on any Home world, according to each signatory's beliefs.

15. Contact with interdicted species or colonies is prohibited.

16. Economic pressure may not be applied to any Home world, and may not extend to the point of injury to any member colony. (Economic war is prohibited.)

17. Interdicted or limited contact of a Home world or colony may be disregarded in the case of extreme jeopardy, whether due to attack, or medical emergency, without pre-approval, with the concurrence and assistance of at least one other Compact member.

NOTE:
    Known species: 35
    Members of Compact: 28
    Of the 7 species not members of the Compact, one is extinct and one has applied for membership, which is at the pre-pending stage. The others are either independent or otherwise unwilling to join. (Two are essentially interdicted.)

RULES OF SETTLEMENT

As agreed in the Compact between Species, colonial settlement by any species must abide by the following rules:

1. Colonies may be established only on worlds without indigenous intelligent life or indigenous proto-intelligent life forms, by Compact definition and examination.
2. Colonies must adhere exactly to Ecological Balances as set forth in those documents by that name, including but not limited to the issues of introduction of alien and bio-engineered species; limitations on development and growth; admixture of cultures, species and ecologies; mineral exploitation limits; biosphere exploitation limits; and technological limits.
3. Fair and Balanced Economies must be developed in advance of settlement.
4. Colony must establish and maintain at least one Oracle installation, which will oversee colonization research.
5. Colony must establish and maintain at least one Oversight organization, as religious or political or military, to enforce the Compact, and to enforce and adjust as needed the Rules of Settlement, Ecological Balances, and Fair and Balanced Economies.
6. Colony must undergo Compact inspection and Oracle Report on an annual basis for 50 years, on a ten-annum basis for 200 years, and centennially thereafter, based on Cuy Native Annum timescale.
7. Deviations from Rules of Settlement will result in complete expulsion of population from that site, in eternum, by Compact forces.
8. These Rules of Settlement shall never apply in the Home system of any species.

FAIR & BALANCED ECONOMIES

1. Restricts the exports of each nation to four primary and up to four secondary items.

2. Each has a specialization based on weather, soil, minerals, and terrain available.

3. Limits on exploitation of natural resources (see specific mineral or resource)

4. Limited trade (see 1, above); shipping is held for nations with few natural resources

5. Manufacturing is allowed on a *very* limited basis, intended to provide vital necessities, and offers a trade item for those with few natural resources.

6. Nations may grow any of these products for local consumption but not export, unless specifically licensed.

The equator of Azureign goes across Maladh, southern Lhasa, central Kendai and the Inner Sea,
        through central Tehassa.
Ring Shadow crosses portions of southern Jia and Farnesse during certain seasons.

Specific Licenses on Azureign (see next page)

AZUREIGN'S FAIR AND BALANCED ECONOMY
as set by the High Priestess at Ysen

Nation/District	Major exports	Minor exports
Lynly	timber, shipping, woodcraft	goats, mushrooms, shellfish
Vai Tilden	wheat, vegetables, fruits	some Inner Sea shipping
Yent	rye, barley, cattle, bodhaata	dragons, tea, timber
Queensland	timber, minerals, ceramics	berries, plass modeling
Maladh	plass, rice, linen	copper, shellfish
Lhasa	grains, cattle, horses	leather, cheese, plass
Kendai	plass, wheat, corn, oats	lime, silica, gymbals
Tehassa	shipping, fruits & vegetables	hardwoods
Farnesse	camels, horses, gymbals	oats, iron, bamboo, bananas
Jia	rice, fish, horses	gold, silver
Misc. Independent or with local oversight		
Archipelago	nuts, fish, shellfish	woven goods (baskets, bags)
Xian (Jia)	rice, bamboo, bananas	coffee
Droda	bamboo, specialty timber	coffee, shellfish
Ñuzco (Lynly)	nuts, timber, specialty cloth	mushrooms
The Lion (Queensland)	furs, fish, yaks	art, textiles

Acknowledgments

The teardrop art used to represent the Ayi spaceships and landers on Reith's Intervals, is:
Drop
https://thenounproject.com/term/drop/715766/
Drop by iconsphere from the Noun Project
Height 582. 1940 dpi. Width 4850. Paid license.

The balloon art used for Zeden's chapter headings is:
Adventure
https://thenounproject.com/term/adventure/2674299/
Adventure by Turkkub from the Noun Project
Height 447. 1490 dpi. Width 3725. Paid license.

Cover art is by Joy Oestreicher and Jason Schumacher, using NASA photographs of Earth and Saturn

Many thanks to my first readers: John, Jennie, Don and Samantha...
...who found conundrums, confusions and a complexity of errors in the first version of The Compact Shatters.

About the Author

Joy Oestreicher is a rare creature: a *third* generation *native Californian.* She loves geography and geology, deserts, fields, grasslands and forests, the foundations of the natural world.

As many writers are, she is a cat person. Meaning she is owned by Moshi (an old man at 13 years) and Zoomie, who is a playful three-year-old, and two new kittens. Joy and her husband are permitted to live in the cats' castle in the southern California desert.

Joy has written several tales set on Azureign and in the Azureign universe, one of which ("Vet-o-Saurus,") appears as a short story in *A Starfarer's Dozen,* from Harcourt Brace, edited by Michael Stearns, 1995.

Also available are other Azureign novels:
Legends of Azureign: Dragon and Oracle, 2018.
Legends of Azureign: Raka and Secrets, 2020.
Legends of Azureign: The Pirate Queen, 2021.

As co-author, Joy had written with D. Oestreicher, these speculative fictions in the "Pandemic Mysteries" series:
Plague of Equals, 2014
Darwin's Paradox, 2017
The Two Pearls, 2020

and historical fiction in the Suramarti Saga:
Kitane, Bull Jumper, 2018
The Murders, The Mosque, 2021

All from Omega Cat Press.

www.ingramcontent.com/pod-product-compliance
Lightning Source LLC
Chambersburg PA
CBHW061202170626
46809CB00003B/1209